Weekly Reader Children's Book Club presents

The Ghost
of Padre Island

THE GHOST
OF
PADRE
ISLAND

by Elizabeth Silverthorne

illustrated by
Dennis Anderson

Nashville • Abingdon Press • New York

THE GHOST OF PADRE ISLAND

Library of Congress Catalog No: 74-13180

SILVERTHORNE, ELIZABETH. The Ghost of Padre Island. SUMMARY:
Mysterious occurrences during a vacation spent in search for a lost Indian
site lead a family of four to treasure and the identity of a ghost.
[1. Mystery and detective stories] I. Anderson, Dennis, illus. II. Title.
PZ7 .S5883Gh   [Fic]

ISBN 0-687-14221-0

Weekly Reader Children's Book Club Edition

To Ivy and Velvet

Contents

chapter 1

A MIDNIGHT VISITOR

The station wagon came to a stop in a large flat area surrounded by sand dunes, and a ball of black fur sailed out.

"Kee-ow, kee-ow," screamed the sea gulls as the ball of fur became a black basset hound that raced into their midst baying in a deep voice.

"Henrietta, come back here!" a chorus of voices called as the other occupants of the car climbed out.

"Padre Island, here we come!" Chuck Merritt, a sandy-haired boy of about eleven years, scrambled out of the car yanking off his tennis shoes at the same time. "Oh, boy, look at those waves. I can't wait to get in them."

Chuck's cousin Roger looked at the endless, rolling mass of water in awe. His thick glasses made his brown eyes seem huge. "So that's the Gulf of Mexico. It's—it's, well, it's a lot bigger than I expected."

"I can't wait to start hunting shells." Chuck's eight-year-old sister, Judy, swung her long, blond pigtails right and left as she scanned the beach. "But what are those funny looking things out in the water that look like bugs with long legs?" She pointed to some platforms out in the Gulf.

"Those are oil drilling rigs, Judy," her mother answered from where she was beginning to unload the station wagon. "There are quarters for the crews on them."

"Come on, gang," she added. "I know we all want to get in the water after the long ride from Austin, so let's hurry and get camp set up."

9

In a few minutes the camping gear had been unloaded, and Roger and Chuck were fitting together the metal poles to hold up the two tents. "Let's make sure the stakes are in good," said Chuck. "I remember the wind can get pretty strong sometimes."

"Say, Chuck," said Roger when the tents were secured.

"Yeah?"

"Where's the bathroom?"

Chuck laughed at his city cousin. Roger lived in Dallas where his father was an accountant, and this was the first time he had been on a camping trip.

"It's do-it-yourself, my friend. We're about to build it right now."

"Build it?"

"Right." Chuck picked up some pieces of board, an old tarpaulin, and a small shovel out of the camping gear. "Follow me." He led the way a short distance from camp behind some sheltering dunes. In a little while Chuck and Roger had fashioned a neat latrine and fastened the tarpaulin to driftwood stakes for privacy.

Chuck was glad his father had taught him so much about camping before he died. A familiar pang of sadness struck Chuck as he remembered other camping trips with his father. But, as his mother said, the only thing to do was be glad they'd had so many good times together.

While Chuck and Roger gathered a good supply of driftwood for fires, Mrs. Merritt and Judy stowed the food, clothing, and other supplies in and around the tents. A cooking table was set up to one side with the portable stove next to it.

Then they all went for a swim in the surf. Henrietta tried to outrace the white-capped waves as they pelted toward the shore. They laughed as they watched her paddle her short legs furiously only to be caught in a breaker and ducked under the salty water.

When they'd had enough swimming, Mrs. Merritt fixed supper on the portable stove.

"I don't know when I've ever been so hungry, Aunt Lucy,"

said Roger as he devoured hamburger stew, fresh tomatoes, bread and butter, and milk and cookies.

His aunt smiled at him. "That's what good fresh air and exercise will do for you."

After supper, the family sat around the driftwood fire that felt good now that the sun had set. Moving strings of lights marked the passage of shrimp boats, and the giant oil drilling rigs were jeweled with light.

Roger was studying his paperback *Guide to Padre Island*. "Padre is a perfect example of a barrier island," he read.

"What's a barrier island?" demanded Judy, who loved new words, even if she didn't always use them quite right.

"Well, I guess it's like an obstacle. Ships can't reach the Texas coast—except by going around it or through channels cut in it." Roger looked at his aunt questioningly.

"That's right, Roger," she said. "The action of the waves and sand built the island."

"Why is it called 'Padre'?" Judy wanted to know.

Roger flipped to the first page of the *Guide*. "It was named after a Spanish priest who built a ranch here around 1800. In Spanish padre means father."

"Thank you, professor," said Chuck. "But I'm more interested in the treasure ships that were wrecked here. They were loaded with gold and jewelry the Spanish stole from the Aztecs. A lot of it was never found. And I'm going to start looking for it first thing tomorrow!"

His mother leaned forward in her deck chair and stirred the fire. "Just think, some of the Spanish explorers may have sat in this very spot around a driftwood fire like ours."

"Or soldiers from the Mexican War or the Civil War," added Roger. "They were both here."

"And pirates and smugglers—maybe they buried some treasure near this spot, too," said Chuck.

"Don't forget why we chose Padre Island for our vacation," Mrs. Merritt reminded them. "The Karankawa Indians probably sat around campfires, too, when they weren't chasing each other or the Spanish explorers."

Chuck knew his mother was referring to her job as an anthropologist. Aside from enjoying a camping trip with the family, she hoped to uncover some more definite clues about the cannibal Indians who had lived on the island.

"Sure," Chuck said, "maybe they sat right here gnawing on the bones of some of the missionaries." He acted out the part of an Indian chewing on a bone and throwing it to a dog. "Here, Henrietta, some for you."

But Henrietta wasn't there to catch the imaginary bone. Chuck whistled, but no dog appeared.

Judy stood up and called, "Henrietta, Henrietta, come here, right now!"

"Maybe she's found some cannibals to share bones with," suggested Roger.

His aunt touched his arm. "Roger, you're worrying Judy." She stood up and looked down the moonlit beach. "Come to think of it, I haven't seen the dog since I fed her a couple of hours ago."

Tears welled in Judy's blue eyes. "M-m-maybe the cannibals are eating Henrietta," she wailed.

"I don't think you have to worry," said Roger. "It must be almost two hundred years since there were . . ." But Chuck and Judy had rushed off before he could finish.

"Here, girl! Here, girl! Henrietta! Henrietta!" Their cries and whistles bounced back and forth among the dunes.

At last Chuck spotted the black dog far around the line of dunes that formed a semicircle behind their camp. He called, and she strolled over to him.

"It's funny," he said as they came back into the family circle. "I'm almost sure someone or something was with her when I first saw her. 'Course, the light's not too good behind the dunes. It looked almost like a . . . but it couldn't have been."

"A what?" asked Judy and Roger together.

"Well, like a pigmy," answered Chuck. He bent to pat Henrietta to hide his embarrassment.

Judy gasped, and Roger chuckled. "More likely it was a calf. There are still cattle on the island, you know."

"Perhaps it was another dog or a coyote," suggested his mother. "Moonlight is tricky." She pushed the sandy lock of hair out of his eyes. "And you do have a good imagination, Chuck."

They all went to bed soon after that. Chuck slept soundly until something in the middle of the night made him jerk wide awake. He stared blindly into the darkness. He tried to sit up and felt a stab of panic. Something was holding him! All he could do was raise his head. Then he remembered.

"Dope," he muttered. "I forgot about the sleeping bag." Quickly he pulled the zipper and raised himself on his elbow. As his eyes grew used to the blackness, he could make out Roger nestled peacefully in a sleeping bag on his cot a few feet away. Except for an occasional snorkling sound caused by his sinus trouble, he was breathing deeply and quietly. So it wasn't Roger who had awakened him. Then who could it have been?

Chuck was sure someone had been moving around in the tent. He checked the luminous dial of his watch—ten minutes past twelve.

He frowned in concentration. Something was different than it had been when he and Roger lay awake making plans to go treasure hunting the next day.

Chuck remembered listening to the lapping of the waves and the distant, long, sad howls of the coyotes—and something else. Chuck pulled himself up to a sitting position. He had it— he had watched the moonlight streaming in the tent opening. Roger had said it was almost like having a light on inside the tent. And now there was no light. The tent was pitch dark because the door flap was closed.

Chuck slipped out of his sleeping bag and through the tent entrance. Outside, he stumbled over a dark lump. "Yike," complained the lump.

"Sorry, old girl. Forgot you were there," Chuck patted Henrietta. He'd forgotten she was sleeping on her favorite blanket just outside their tent. She thumped her tail sleepily.

"Well, anyway," thought Chuck. "She didn't bark at whoever woke me up." He glanced at the other tent. "I'd better check on Mom and Judy."

The canvas folds that formed the door of the tent were hooked securely to its sides. Standing in the doorway, Chuck could see clearly the outlines of his mother and Judy on their cots. Next to Judy's blond head was a small mound that Chuck knew was her favorite doll, Betsy Ann. It was certain neither of them had been roaming around in the last few minutes. Puzzled, Chuck seated himself on a driftwood log near the ashes of the campfire they had sat around earlier that evening.

Henrietta came over to lie down beside him. Watching the moonlit waves curl onto the shore, Chuck remembered how good it had felt to splash in them after driving a third of the way across Texas.

"We're lucky, Hen," he said, "that Mom has a job that takes us to such great places. The only thing that would be better is if Dad were still with us, too." Henrietta moved closer and leaned her head against his knee. "You miss him, too, don't you?"

It had been a little over a year since Chuck's father had been killed in an airplane crash while on a field trip. He had been an archeologist. Chuck smiled to himself as he thought of how many times he'd had to explain to people about both his parents being doctors, but not the kind who take care of sick people.

A coyote howled in the distance. Chuck shivered and looked behind him. He had the feeling someone was watching. But there was nothing in sight except the white, ripply dunes covered with dark patches which he knew were wild grasses and vines.

"Probably some old cow giving me the once over from behind a dune," he muttered.

But the breeze off the water suddenly seemed colder, and he hurried to get back into the warmth of his sleeping bag.

chapter 2

A DISCOVERY

Next morning Henrietta was the first one up, trying to teach the sea gulls further lessons. Chuck heard her barking through the tail end of his last dream. "Maybe she thinks the early dog catches the bird," he thought.

Opening one eye, he saw that Roger was still buried in his sleeping bag. Chuck was glad Roger could come on this trip. He knew that his cousin spent a lot of time indoors reading and that Roger's parents hoped the time on Padre Island would make Roger stronger, so he wouldn't always be having colds and sinus trouble.

Chuck jumped up and shook Roger's cot. "Come on, Rog, let's go swimming."

"Uh, it might be cold," muttered Roger. He burrowed down deeper into his sleeping bag.

"Come on, sissy." Chuck gave Roger a shove that almost jarred him off the cot. "Last one in is a jellyfish."

The two were soon splashing in the somersaulting waves. As Chuck watched the sun touch the waves with light and turn the distant dunes into sparkling rock candy hills, he decided he wouldn't mention his midnight awakening. Everything seemed so normal this morning, and he didn't have any proof to offer. Also, he didn't care to think about pigmies anymore.

At first the water was chilly, but after a few minutes of brisk swimming, they warmed up. "I can't get used to the salt," sputtered Roger as a wave washed over his head.

"Sure beats the chlorine in swimming pools," said Chuck.

"See how easy it is to float." He flopped over on his back to demonstrate. As he watched his toes, a bigger than usual wave washed over his face, leaving him sputtering.

Roger laughed. "That's something else you don't have in pools."

A few minutes later he pointed to the shore where Judy had come to the edge of the water and was waving her arms. "Guess we'd better go in."

"I'm going to ride in," Chuck announced. He waited until a wave was at the top of its crest and threw himself face down on it. As the wave broke and rolled toward shore it took him with it. When that wave ran out of steam, he caught another bigger one that swept him all the way up onto the shore.

Roger looked on enviously. "That looks like fun." He tried to catch several waves but waited too long or lunged too soon. In disgust he gave up and walked to the beach.

"You just need to practice," Chuck said. Although Roger was exactly a year older—both their birthdays fell on April 3, and this year Roger turned twelve and Chuck eleven—this was the first time he had been to Padre Island.

Mrs. Merritt had orange juice and milk, toast, and scrambled eggs with bacon chipped up in them ready for the swimmers.

"Mmmm, why don't we ever have eggs fixed like this at home?" asked Chuck.

"Yes," said the always hungry Judy. "They're 'specially good."

"I don't know. I never think of fixing eggs this way at home. It just seems to be a camping dish," answered Mrs. Merritt. "Maybe that's why it tastes so 'specially good.'"

She looked around at the children. "Well, what does everyone want to do today? I'm going to sunbathe and reread some of the reference material I brought on the Karankawa Indians. My map indicates that an old camping site for that tribe may have been in this area. But because of the way the dunes shift and change the configuration of the land, no one has been able to locate it."

"Roger and I are going treasure hunting," announced Chuck.

"Me, too." Judy looked hopefully at her brother.

"Oh, no," groaned Chuck. "You're too little."

"Now, Chuck," began his mother.

Knowing what was coming, Chuck said quickly, "O.K., we'll take you this one time. But you have to keep up and not be stopping to pick up dumb shells every minute."

"Can Henrietta come, too?" asked Judy.

"Of course," answered Chuck, much more willingly. "She ought to be good at finding treasure. Remember when we took her to the lake? She found clams where we couldn't see any signs of them."

Roger looked surprised, and Chuck explained. At the lake Henrietta would go sniffing along the shore. Then she would stop and start digging furiously in the sand. In a few seconds she would turn up a good big clam.

"This is the first time I ever knew a clam hound," Roger chuckled.

Shortly after breakfast the treasure hunters started. Chuck carried one of his mother's small trowels that he'd borrowed for digging. Over his shoulder he had slung a canteen of water. Roger had a compass, a first aid kit, and his paperback copy of *Guide to Padre Island*.

Carefully folded and concealed in the pocket of her blouse, Judy had a small paper sack. "Just in case" there should be some irresistible shells along their path.

She also had stowed in her blue jeans pocket a piece of left-over toast, wrapped in a paper napkin. Dr. Merritt often said that Judy's greatest fear was that she would be caught between meals without provisions and starve to death.

In spite of the fact that she had no idea where they were going, Henrietta, as usual, insisted on being the leader of the group.

As soon as they got a little way from camp they discovered that while many of the dunes were covered with wild grasses, shells, and pieces of driftwood, others were pure white sand. They reminded Chuck of pictures of ski slopes he had seen.

Holding two long pieces of driftwood under his arms in imitation of skiers' poles, he zigged and zagged down the smooth side of a tall dune. "Look at me! I'm skiing!" he called. As he neared the bottom, his momentum sent him head over heels, and he landed in a laughing heap in the soft sand.

Soon all three children were slipping and sliding down the sandy slopes. Judy preferred to do her skiing sitting down. Even the dignified Henrietta joined in the action. With her black, shiny fur she looked like a seal as she slid, barking, down the dunes.

Chuck found a piece of flat board they could use as a sled. Taking turns, they rode it lying on their stomachs or in a kneeling position. With Judy holding her, Henrietta joined the sledding, too.

After nearly an hour Chuck said, "Hey, gang, we're never going to find any treasure this way. Let's get back to business."

For a long time the three trudged along seriously, heads down, eyes scanning the ground. While they were sand-skiing, they had removed the sandals Mrs. Merritt had insisted they wear. Now at each step the sand scrunched up deliciously between their toes.

They kicked hopefully at each little mound of sand. Several times Chuck stopped the expedition to dig with the trowel. Once, to his disgust, he turned up a pile of beer cans and an old piece of a tire.

"Look what I found!" called Judy, holding up a large, perfect sand dollar. Roger had never seen one before. He examined the star design on the white cover of the shell.

"Let's open it and show Roger the five little shells inside that look like birds," said Chuck.

"No," said Judy, "I might not find another perfect one."

"O.K., if that's the way you want to be about it," said Chuck.

"Well, if we find another one we'll open it," Judy promised.

As they went along, Henrietta upset the sand crab population of the island by sniffing out and digging up a number of the peacefully resting creatures. At least she did until one old grandfather crab, instead of scuttling away, reached out and grabbed her nose.

"Yip, yip, yip!" She scrambled back to the children, howling and dragging the stubborn old crab with her.

"Let go, you meanie, let go!" shouted Judy, trying to knock the crab off with a piece of driftwood.

Chuck and Roger couldn't help laughing even though they knew Henrietta was suffering. "Don't, Judy. Let me get it," said Chuck. Gently he forced open the powerful pincers.

For a minute the fierce old crab sat still, looking as though he wanted to get a fresh grip on Henrietta's nose. Judy nudged him with her stick, saying "Shoo, shoo!"

At that he began to move slowly away sideways, keeping his bulging eyes on the enemy until he was out of sight. After having cold water from the canteen applied to her sore nose and receiving loving care from Judy, Henrietta was ready to continue the hunt.

From time to time Roger took careful bearings with his compass. Since there were few landmarks to use for guides, it would be easy to get confused and lost in the dunes. Realizing this, Dr. Merritt had called their attention to the tall, weather-beaten pole near their camp. This pole had apparently been used to fly weather flags in earlier times. It was so high that it was easy to spot from a long distance.

As they were plodding up and down a series of tightly clustered dunes, Chuck said, "This is a lot better than going for a walk at home."

"You bet," agreed Roger, "'cause here you never know what you'll find over the next dune." As he spoke they reached the top of an especially high dune.

"Well, I'll be," said Chuck. All four stopped and stared.

"It's a little house," said Judy.

In front of them, nestled in among the dunes was a small building. But it wasn't really a house. In fact, it looked something like the shack Chuck and his friends had built for a clubhouse on a vacant lot back home.

As they approached it, Chuck saw why the building looked like his clubhouse. It, too, was built of odd size pieces and bits of boards. Although it might look like a design for a crazy quilt, this building was snugly built. There were no gaps in the boards. Two windows were neatly set in on each side, and each window had shutters hooked to the siding.

Weather-beaten barrels stood at two corners of the house to catch rain. The sidewalk was a path of sand outlined neatly in multicolored shells.

"Oh, how pretty," exclaimed Judy. "Someone nice must live here."

"I think I'll ring the bell," said Chuck.

"Wait," said Roger, "maybe we shouldn't. Maybe whoever lives here wouldn't want to be disturbed."

"It wouldn't hurt just to ask them which is the best direction to go to look for treasure," said Chuck. He yanked the bell's rope, setting off a loud "clang, clang."

Minutes passed and nothing happened, so Chuck gave the door a firm rap. To his surprise it swung open.

The three stuck their heads into the opening. In the dim light nobody was to be seen. Henrietta, who couldn't see a thing through all their legs, squeezed herself between Roger and Judy and ran barking into the middle of the room.

"Hello, hello," called a high-pitched voice. Startled, the trio almost fell into the room.

"Look," laughed Roger, pointing. In the far corner was a bright green parrot in a cage.

"Hello," said the bird again. "How about a little drink, mate?"

"Hello, yourself," said Judy going over to him. "What a funny cage you have."

Roger joined her. "It's handmade. Look, the bars are made of plaited rope, and the thick bottom and this carved top are made out of pieces of driftwood."

The occupant of the cage cocked his head and watched them with his bright eyes. "Yo ho ho. A little rum. A little rum," he chanted.

"Sorry, chum," said Chuck. "All we have is water, and you already have some of that." He pointed to one of the shell dishes in the cage.

The children looked around the room curiously. "It's like a ship's cabin," said Chuck in delight.

For a bed there was a hammock, and for lights, ship's lanterns hung from the ceiling. The table had a rim around it. Chuck explained that was to keep dishes from sliding around when a ship got into rough water.

Ship's lockers and barrels served for storage. Odd chests and boxes provided seating and additional storage space. On the back of the door hung pieces of rope of all sizes and also several life preservers.

"Those look like Christmas ornaments," said Judy in wonder. She was pointing to some ropes of colored glass balls hanging on one wall.

"I saw some like them in a souvenir shop in Corpus Christi once," said Chuck. "The lady said the Japanese used them for fishing net floats. Sometimes they wash up on the beach."

Roger nodded. "I read about them in my guidebook. Sometimes it takes them twenty or twenty-five years to float here all the way from Japanese fishing waters."

Chuck whistled. "Wow, imagine that!"

"I just know someone nice lives here now," said Judy, "everything is so neat, and the balls are such a pretty decoration." The three children moved closer to the colored balls for a better look.

Suddenly a booming voice made them jump. "So! What's the meaning of this? Trespassing on private property, eh? Who's responsible for breaking into my house?"

Their hearts pounding, the three children turned to face their questioner.

Almost filling the doorway stood a huge man with a reddish beard and eyebrows. A fringe of red hair outlined his bald head. His voice sounded like thunder to the terrified intruders, and his stormy eyes seemed to flash blue lightning at them.

Chuck saw with horrified fascination that the arm he raised to shake at them ended not in a fist—but in a hook!

chapter 3

THE CASE
OF THE MISSING BROWNIES

Roger stood with his mouth hanging open like a drawer he had forgotten to close. Judy took a quick step backward so she was behind Roger. Henrietta wriggled behind Judy. Chuck realized that someone had to speak up, and it looked as though he was the one.

"We're s-sorry, mister. H-honestly, we didn't mean to trespass." Chuck took a deep breath to steady his voice, which sounded shakier than he wanted it to. "You see we were hunting for treasure and saw your shack—I mean your house— so I rang the bell, and nobody answered; so I knocked and the door sort of came open, and we heard a voice, and it turned out to be a parrot, and we were just looking around."

Chuck stopped for breath, and Roger added helpfully, "It's so interesting. Just like a ship."

"I 'specially like the Christmas tree balls and your beautiful parrot," Judy chimed in. "Does he have a name?"

"Of course, he has a name." The stormy scowl softened a little. "It's Mr. Bones."

"A little drink for Mr. Bones. A little drink for Mr. Bones," chanted the bird.

"Is that all he talks about?" began Judy. A nudge from Chuck stopped her. Just when the stranger was cooling down a little, he didn't want his dumb sister to insult his bird and make him angry again.

Chuck thought the best thing they could do was to leave as quickly as possible. He spoke to Roger and Judy, "I think we'd

better be getting back to camp for lunch now. Mom will be worried about us."

Turning to the stranger he said, "Please excuse us for barging into your house, sir. We really didn't mean to."

"Well, I guess you didn't mean no harm, not like some of those others. But you remember now. This here is private property, and don't come breaking in here again." The man's voice was still gruff, but he was no longer frowning.

As they filed out, Henrietta stopped a minute to look into the stranger's face. She wagged her tail hesitantly as if asking forgiveness for her part in the intrusion. Chuck was almost sure he saw the light blue eyes of the large man crinkle a little.

It was hard for anyone to look at Henrietta without smiling. Judy said her sad eyes and wagging tail made her seem happy at one end and unhappy at the other. For a second Chuck thought the man was going to reach out and touch the dog. However, the stranger merely turned away to put his fishing tackle up on a shelf near the front door and said, "Run on now. Go on back to where you belong."

"Cheez, what a grouch," said Chuck as soon as they were out of the man's hearing.

"Yeah, a *gen-u-ine* grouch," echoed Judy.

"But he was right, you know. We were trespassing. For all he knew we might have been going to steal some of his stuff," Roger said.

"Aw, baloney." Chuck sent a shell spinning with his toe. "Do we *look* like criminals?"

Roger kept his eyes on the sand and didn't answer. Chuck wanted to apologize for sounding ruder than he meant to. But he felt tired, hungry, and vaguely discouraged, so he said nothing.

The hike back to camp was made in silence except for Henrietta and Judy. At a safe distance Henrietta yapped at the pale, square-shelled ghost crabs that scuttled across their path. Sometimes she barked back at ground squirrels who stopped to scold them before diving into their burrows. Judy let out a few excited squeals when she found shells of a pretty shape or color.

All of them were glad to reach camp. Mrs. Merritt reported that she had walked to a little grocery store near the entrance of the camping area for milk and bread and that she had also called her sister in Corpus Christi. "I wanted to let her and Uncle John know that we arrived on Padre safely and that we'd be coming to spend a few days with them on our way home. Aunt Mabel was so pleased that Roger is with us."

"Wasn't she pleased about Chuck and me and Henrietta coming, too?" demanded Judy.

"Well, she said she'd try to stand it," teased Dr. Merritt. "Now, everybody, lunch is do-it-yourself." She pointed to the serving table where she had laid out deviled ham, cheese, peanut butter and crackers, plus apples and milk.

Watching the children eating in almost complete silence, her blue eyes grew puzzled.

"Did you get too much sun today?" she asked. "Judy, you do look a little pink."

"The sun wasn't too hot, Mom. It's just that we got into a strange *perdicament,*" answered Judy.

"Predicament, dear," said her mother. "That sounds interesting. Tell me about it."

The three children joined in describing the details of their discovery of the little ship-like cabin and their meeting with the unfriendly island native.

"He's probably an old sailor turned beachcomber," said Dr. Merritt. "You really shouldn't have walked into his house. If he doesn't want company, that's his right. Just be sure you keep out of his way and don't bother him any more."

"Don't worry. I'll be happy not to *ever* see him again," said Chuck.

When the lunch things had been cleared away, Mrs. Merritt declared a siesta time. Judy settled in her tent to examine and clean her shells, and Mrs. Merritt stretched out on her cot to read and doze.

Chuck got out his cards and offered to teach Roger a couple of his best card tricks. Soon the boys were back on friendly terms again, and the unpleasantness of the morning was forgotten.

In the later part of the afternoon the whole family went dune-skiing. The children showed Mrs. Merritt what they had learned about the new sport, and soon she was zigging and zagging down the dunes as well as any of them.

After a while she said, "How about catching our dinner for tonight? I saw some fish jumping a little way out in the surf this afternoon."

"Sure," both boys chorused.

"I'd better stay with Henrietta so she won't bark and scare the fish," said Judy.

So while Mrs. Merritt and the boys waded out to surf-fish with their rods and reels, Judy threw pieces of driftwood into the water for Henrietta. The black dog splashed through the surf until she caught the wood and then rode the waves back to shore holding her head high.

Chuck showed Roger how to cast his line without fouling his reel. Every few minutes the silvery body of a fish would flash out of the water and shine in the rays of the setting sun. Then it would disappear into the water with a slight plop.

Mrs. Merritt caught the first fish—a good-sized trout—and then Roger caught one and lost it because he didn't reel in steadily enough. Chuck caught two trout, his mother one more, and finally Roger caught one and managed to reel it in. When they had five fish stowed in the canvas sling that Chuck carried over his shoulder, Mrs. Merritt said it was time to quit.

That evening, dinner was a feast of grilled trout baked in hot coals. As they ate they watched the shrimp boats passing on the far horizon where they were outlined against the deeper blue of the sky.

"I've fixed Chuck and Judy's favorite dessert, Roger. I hope you like it, too," said Mrs. Merritt. She got up and went back to the folding table near the large tent.

"Well, I'll declare!" she exclaimed. Coming back to the group with a pan in her hand she asked, "O.K., who's the joker?"

"What's the matter, Mom?" asked Chuck.

"Why, somebody's taken a couple of brownies and left a coin in their place!"

Roger laughed. "Well, if they're paid for, no great crime has been committed."

"But—but, I've never seen a coin like this except in books!" exclaimed Mrs. Merritt. Her reddish-blond hair glinted in the firelight as she stooped by the fire to get a better light on the coin.

The others crowded around her to get a look at the strange piece of money. It had once been round, but now its edges were ragged and out of shape. On one side were pictured columns rising out of clouds. On the other were a number of tiny pictures.

"I see some animals—a lion and some snakes," said Judy.

"And both sides have funny words and numbers on them," said Chuck.

"It might be an ancient Spanish coin," suggested Roger.

"Yes," said Dr. Merritt, who had put on her glasses and was turning the coin over, examining the markings closely. "I believe you're right, Roger. I think this is a Mexican two-real piece; it was one of the first coins to be made in what the Spanish called the New World."

"How old would it be, Mom?" asked Chuck, eagerly.

His mother thought for a minute. "At least four hundred years."

Roger let out his breath in a long whistle. He had been a coin collector for years. His eyes shone. "It must be worth a fortune!"

"Well, maybe not a fortune. But it is a valuable coin." Mrs. Merritt shook her head. "How in the world did it get into my brownie pan?"

"How long has the pan been on the table?" asked Roger.

"I baked the brownies in the portable oven this morning before lunch. When they were cool I put the plastic lid on them. They've been there since then."

"And you were suspicious of one of us?" said Judy.

"Well, yes, when I saw that there were two brownies missing and a coin where they had been, I thought one of you had played a trick."

Around the campfire that night the case of the missing brownies was the main topic of conversation. Roger suggested pack rats or crows that leave objects in exchange for what they take.

But Mrs. Merritt was quite sure that the plastic cover had been firmly on the pan before and after the exchange. "Even if an animal or bird could have worked the cover off, I'm certain they wouldn't have replaced it," she added.

Chuck turned the coin over in the firelight. "Maybe Jean Lafitte or some of his men handled this coin," he said. "There's a chapter in Roger's book that tells about them burying a lot of treasure under a large round rock."

"Did anybody find it?" asked Judy.

"Not that we know of," said Roger. "On the rock they carved 'Dig Deeper.' Some kids found a rock like that here once. But when they tried to bring their parents back to show it to them, they couldn't find it."

"And then it might not have been pirate loot; it might have come from a shipwreck," mused Chuck. "Look in the *Guide,* Rog, and read us that part again about the big shipwreck."

From his pocket, Roger pulled out the guidebook, which was beginning to be a little dog-eared.

"Let me see," he peered through his thick glasses at the pages. "Here it is. In 1553 twenty Spanish ships sailed out of Vera Cruz, Mexico, headed for Spain."

"Tell the part about the storm," urged Chuck.

"That's next," said Roger. "'A terrible storm came up, and more than half of them were shipwrecked on Padre Island.'" He ran his finger on down the page. "And it says that coins from those wrecked ships and from others keep turning up here whenever the sands shift."

"Well, whether our coin came from pirate loot or from a shipwreck still doesn't explain how it got in my brownie pan!" said Mrs. Merritt.

Long after the others were asleep Chuck and Roger lay awake whispering. The strange coin had made them eager to get on with their own treasure hunting.

They decided to get an early start to carry out their carefully made plans. Tomorrow they would conduct a really scientific search just as archeologists do when carrying out an archeological project.

The soothing breeze and the murmur of the waves finally lulled them to sleep.

Chuck's dreams were full of pirates and treasure chests and sunken ships. Once he thought he saw Mr. Bones sitting on top of a large round rock singing:

Fifteen men on a dead man's chest
Yo ho ho and a bottle of rum!

chapter 4

LOST!

The next morning after a quick swim and breakfast Chuck and Roger gathered digging equipment and poles for probing.

Today, Chuck explained to his mother, they were going to hunt scientifically. "First we'll mark off a square on the sand. Then we'll step off and probe every foot of the square before we move on."

Roger had also discovered some tips for finding treasure in his guidebook.

"We've got to look for beeswax," he announced.

"What does beeswax have to do with treasure?" demanded Judy, looking up from the buttered biscuit she was sharing with Henrietta.

"The ships carried huge hunks of it for making candles," explained Roger. "And they also used it for treating the thread they used to sew sails."

"And we'd better keep an eye out for pieces of lead with square nail holes in them, too," he added. "They were used on the bottoms of ships so the barnacles would get lead poisoning. Then the sailors wouldn't have to work so hard scraping them off."

Chuck looked at Roger with envy. Being a bookworm paid off sometimes. At least Roger had sense enough to make good use of what he read in books.

Chuck and Roger tried not to look pleased when Judy tossed Henrietta the last crumb of biscuit and said, "Henrietta and I don't want to waste our time poking in the sand turning up old pork and beans cans. We want to hunt for shells. Can we go by ourselves, please, Mom?"

"You two can come with me and hunt shells while I investigate some ancient shell mounds just a little way from here that might indicate an Indian campsite. We'll be back for lunch." She turned to the boys, "And you all plan to be back here by noon, if not before."

A short distance from their campsite the treasure hunters began their operations. Marking off a room-sized area, they slowly walked over every foot of it, probing the sand carefully with their sticks. When nothing more exciting than pieces of shell and driftwood turned up, they moved on to another space.

Again they marked off an area, walked and probed. This time they succeeded in frightening a nest of pocket gophers. The odd little creatures went scurrying and burrowing to escape the monsters who had suddenly invaded their little world.

"Let's sit down a minute," said Roger, who was puffing. "I can use a drink."

"Me, too." Chuck dropped down on a handy piece of driftwood and handed the canteen to Roger. "This treasure hunting is hard work. I feel as if my mouth is full of sand." He broke off and stared hard at a dune a little distance from them.

"Did you see something move over there?" He nodded toward the dune.

"No," answered Roger, "I was looking down at the canteen. What did it look like?"

"It looked like a head," answered Chuck, "and it ducked behind a dune just as I turned toward it."

"Well," said Roger, handing the canteen back to Chuck, "just after we started this morning I looked back and thought I saw something jump behind a dune. I didn't say anything, because it could have been my imagination or a coyote or something."

"Coyotes don't follow people like that," said Chuck firmly. "And I don't believe it's our imagination. That first night I'm sure someone was watching us. Then there was the coin left in the brownie pan last night. And now this morning we're being followed and watched!"

He jumped up. "Come on, Rog. Let's rush it together!" Quickly he ran around one side of the huge dune and motioned Roger to climb through the pass that connected that dune with the next one.

But there was no sign of any eavesdropper behind the dune. And the soft sand refused to reveal the clue of any footprints.

"It's no use," said Roger. He pointed to the two chains of dunes stretching beyond the one they had just crossed. "If anyone is here and doesn't want us to see him, it would be easy for him to hide forever in all those dunes."

Chuck had to agree. "Well, we might as well get back to work," he said.

Two more areas were carefully mapped out and probed by the treasure hunters. Since nothing more exciting than some camper's pile of buried cans turned up, the hungry boys decided to return to camp.

As they trudged along, Chuck tried to evaluate their efforts the way his mother did her research projects. "Well, at least we've eliminated some distance by our work today."

"Sure," said Roger. "This island is 113 miles long. Say we covered half a mile—that leaves us only 112½ miles to go—lengthwise, that is."

"O.K., professor," Chuck grinned at his cousin. "We may just have to make a lifetime career out of this project."

Mrs. Merritt met them as they walked into camp. "Hello, boys, I've got sandwiches ready for lunch. Did you see Judy and Henrietta on your way back?"

"No, Mom," answered Chuck. "We haven't seen them since breakfast. Didn't they go with you?"

"Yes, but Judy wanted to try for shells a little farther away, and then I couldn't find her when I got ready to come back. I called several times. I thought maybe she had found you. It's not like Judy to be late for a meal, you know." His mother gave a tight little smile, and Chuck knew she was trying not to show how worried she was.

"We'll go look for them," he volunteered. Roger nodded.

"All right," said Mrs. Merritt. "Let's spread out and round them up in a hurry. Since you two came from that direction and I came from that one, they must be in the area in back of the camp."

"How far back does the island go?" asked Chuck.

"About two miles back in this area," said Roger, studying the *Guide*.

"But they can't have gone that far," said Mrs. Merritt. "I'll walk this way." She pointed to the southwest. "You boys bear northwest. Let's meet back here in an hour. Surely we will have located them by then. Or they will have found their way back themselves."

Mrs. Merritt's voice was calm, but her face was pale. She quickly found her sunglasses and sun hat and set off.

As they separated, she called back to the boys, "Be careful, fellows. Stay together and watch your landmarks."

"Gee, I've never seen Mom so worried," said Chuck.

"Yes," Roger replied, "I noticed how she looked at the water. But I guess she didn't even want to think they might have gone in that direction."

"Of course not! Anyway, Henrietta has enough sense to stay out of trouble." Chuck wished he felt as sure as he tried to sound. Suddenly he wanted to see his pesky little sister more than he had ever wanted anything in his life. "Come on, Rog, hurry up, can't you?"

The two boys scrambled over and between the endless dunes. Every few minutes they stopped to call Judy or Henrietta. The sun beat fiercely on their bare heads. Impatiently Chuck brushed the unruly lock of hair out of his eyes. He wished he had listened to his mother's advice to wear a hat.

As time passed the sand seemed to get deeper and their feet seemed to get heavier. Each dune seemed a little higher than the one they had just climbed. The shadow of every scrubby bush and wild flower stood out sharply under the beating sun.

Chuck noticed that Roger's face was pale and his forehead beaded with sweat. "Got to slow down," he thought, "can't have Roger getting a sunstroke."

When they had been walking for half an hour, they sat down for a few minutes to get their breath before starting back to camp.

Roger dried the perspiration from his glasses with his shirt. "Bet they're all back in camp right now, gobbling up the lunch."

Chuck knew his cousin was trying to cheer him up. "Hope you're right. I wouldn't even be mad if they ate it all as long as everybody is O.K."

They headed back toward camp in a direction slightly different from the one they had taken as they began their search. They plodded along, stopping to call, then dragging one foot after the other.

When a blacktailed jackrabbit hopped in front of them for a few yards, neither of them paid any attention to it. "Was it just yesterday that I thought hiking through the dunes was fun?" Chuck wondered to himself.

Reaching camp, they found it empty. After drinking thirstily from the water jug, they sat listlessly in the camp chairs under the tarpaulin that served as roof and sun shade.

In a few minutes Dr. Merritt appeared. Her eyes scanned the area eagerly as she approached. Her expression turned to one of weariness when she saw that only Chuck and Roger were there.

While his mother sank into a chair, Chuck ran to get her a drink of water. No one said anything for a few minutes. It made Chuck feel as though a tight rubber band was around his throat to see his mother so pale and sad.

It was the way she had looked for so long after his father's death. He found that he was praying silently: "Please, God, don't let anything happen to Judy. I promise I'll be better and not tease her so much when she says dumb things or uses long words she doesn't understand."

In a few minutes Dr. Merritt stood up and cleared her throat. "I think I'd better get the Rangers to help us. There's a station a few miles up the island. I'm sure Judy has just gotten carried away with her shell collecting and gone too far. But the Rangers know the island better than we do."

She broke off as the usually calm Roger began to sputter, "Well, I'll be . . . would you look . . . look at that!"

Following the direction of his hypnotized stare, the others saw a strange procession trailing into camp.

First came Judy. Her braids had come undone and her shirt was torn and dirty. Tears and dirt had streaked her sunburned face, but she broke into a huge smile when she saw the wide-eyed group staring at her.

Chuck's mouth dropped open when he saw who was following his little sister. It was the cranky red-bearded sailor—and cradled in his arms, as tenderly as if he were a mother and she a baby, he carried Henrietta!

chapter 5

BARNACLE BILL

In a couple of giant steps Lucy Merritt reached her daughter. Laughing and crying at the same time, she hugged her tightly and kissed the dirty, tear-stained face again and again.

"Glad you're O.K., Judy," said Roger, looking at her solemnly.

Chuck only grinned at his eight-year-old sister and said, "Hi," but he felt as if the tight rubber band had been removed from his throat.

While the family greeted Judy, the big stranger gently placed Henrietta on the sand. She ran to each member of the family for her welcome home. She was limping slightly on her left front paw.

When her mother let her go, Judy's words fell over each other as she tried to tell everything at the same time.

"We got lost! And Henrietta fell in a hole. And I called and called and nobody heard me! And Hen and I were both crying. And then he came! Oh, this is Barnacle Bill, everybody. And he's really nice. Not grouchy like we thought. And he lost his hand in a fight with a shark. And he saved Henrietta. But her foot may be sprained . . ."

"Whoa," Dr. Merritt interrupted when it began to seem that Judy would never come to a stop. "Wait a minute. We're very grateful to you, Mr. Barn—er, what is your real name, sir?"

The red-bearded man stepped forward to shake the hand Dr. Merritt extended. "Barnacle Bill is fine. Jones is the last name.

But nobody hardly uses it nowadays."

Mrs. Merritt gave him a warm smile. "We'll never be able to thank you for what you have done for us, Bill. Now you must stay and have some lunch with us."

Almost shyly the big man at first refused. He muttered something about having to get back to his cabin. But when they all begged him to stay he finally gave in.

His eyes twinkled when he found they were having root beer with the sandwiches. "It's my favorite drink, but I only get it rarely."

As they ate Judy and Bill told the others the story of the rescue in detail. She and Henrietta had wandered so far from camp that Judy had become confused and couldn't figure out the way back. The more they walked, the more mixed up she became.

Then Henrietta had fallen into a deep crevice. Judy's arms weren't long enough to reach her to pull her out. For a long time Henrietta had tried to find footholds herself. But the sand always crumbled away under her weight.

"And then she barked for a long time. And I called for help for a long time. But nobody heard us. So Hen lay down in the bottom of the hole and cried. And I thought we'd never see you all again. So I cried, too."

Judy's blue eyes filled with tears again as she remembered how she had felt. Then she smiled as she remembered what happened next.

"That's when Barnacle Bill found us. He got down in the hole and lifted Henrietta out. Then he brought us back to camp." Judy beamed at her new friend as she began on her third sandwich.

When the story was over, Mrs. Merritt began to thank Judy's rescuer again, but she stopped when she saw that she was embarrassing him. Instead, she offered him another can of root beer.

While he drank it, he apologized to the children for frightening them when they had stumbled onto his shack.

"Sometimes campers just wander in and even carry out

some of my stuff," he added.

"Don't you ever lock the door?" asked Roger.

"Don't like to. Don't believe a man oughta have to lock up what's his. Wouldn't have to if people acted like they should."

Chuck felt a little uncomfortable at the reference to their uninvited visit. To change the subject, he asked, "Have you lived on Padre Island long, Mr. Jones?"

"Just call me Bill, son. Never did like things fancy." The old sailor carefully drained the last of his root beer and wiped away a few drops from his beard by running his hook over it.

Bill settled back in his chair. The good food and the friendliness of the Merritts seemed to have a mellowing effect on the old beachcomber.

At last he answered Chuck's question. "Yep, boy. I reckon I've spent all my life that I can remember in and on and by the waters of that big pond." He waved his hook toward the Gulf of Mexico, where the waves were slapping more briskly than usual at the beach.

"My great-great-great grandfather was one of Jean Lafitte's men." Chuck noticed that he seemed proud of that fact. "Yes siree," the old sailor added winking and waving his hook vaguely toward the mainland, "there's many a good, solid family tree in these here parts sprung from those old buccaneers.

"Used to work a shrimp boat myself. Had my own deepwater craft for a while."

"You mean a charter boat to take fishermen out to the deep water where the large fish are?" asked Dr. Merritt.

"Yep, didn't care much for that. Too many Sunday fishing experts trying to tell me how to run my business."

Now, he explained, he was retired. Except for taking a job from time to time with the fishing fleet at Port Aransas to earn a little money for store-bought necessities like coffee, flour, sugar, and root beer. Otherwise, he lived off the island and the Gulf.

The Merritts listened in amazement as he named the foods that were his regular diet. He mentioned more kinds of fish than Chuck had ever heard of. Then there were crabs, ducks, bird and turtle eggs, seaweed, prickly pear fruit, jackrabbits, and rattlesnake steaks.

"Ugh," said Judy.

Bill chuckled, his eyes crinkling up so they seemed almost to disappear. "Now, Miss Judy, don't you go 'ughing' good food. How do you know you don't like something if you ain't never tasted it? A rattlesnake steak roasted just right is darn good eating. Got a real fine flavor, it has."

"How in the world do you manage for fresh water?" asked Mrs. Merritt. She was thinking of the trouble they had hauling in all their drinking, washing, and cooking water.

Bill chuckled again. "One thing I learned. If you'll just work with her, Old Mother Nature'll provide for you pretty good. 'Course I got rain barrels to catch and store rainwater. But when we get a dry spell, there's another way to get water here. The Kronks knew it, but the Spanish explorin' rascals didn't."

"What was it?" asked Roger.

"Well, sir, all you got to do is find a water dune and dig down a few feet. All the sweet water you want. City folks better boil it before drinking," he added a little snobbishly. "Since they got more delicate stomachs than us natives."

"Who were the Kronks?" asked Judy.

"That's the nickname for the Karankawa Indians who lived here a long time ago, isn't it?" asked Roger.

His aunt nodded. "That's right, Roger."

"You mean the cannibals?" demanded Judy.

This time Bill nodded. "That's right, little lady. And a right mean crew they was, too. Some folks excuse them and say they didn't mean no harm. On account of if they was a-slicing you up and a-roasting bits of you and a-eating you in front of your very eyes, it was a part of their religious goings on."

Judy scrambled to her feet. "I think Henrietta and I need to rest for a while," she said. "Come on, girl." Grasping Henrietta's collar firmly she moved off to her tent.

Chuck made a face at Roger. Girls! Scared to hear about exciting stuff that happened hundreds of years ago!

The rest of the family lost track of time as they sat listening to the old sailor tell stories of the early history of the island, stories that had been passed on to him by his father and grandfather.

His light blue eyes assumed a faraway look as he told tales of Spanish explorers, Jean Lafitte and his band of pirates, and rugged settlers who had set up ranches on the island. His listeners would have been happy to sit listening much longer, but Bill suddenly seemed anxious to get back to his cabin.

"Got some things to tend to," he said. "Tell you what, though. If you want to dig around in an old Indian camp, there's one I found a ways up the island that nobody else ain't never explored. If you want me to take you up there tomorrow, ma'am, I will."

"That would be wonderful. It might just be the lost camp I'm looking for!" said Dr. Merritt. "I'd really appreciate your showing it to me."

"Can Rog and I come, too?" Chuck asked. "There might be arrowheads and maybe even some buried treasure."

"And Henrietta and me," Judy added quickly as she rejoined the group. "There might be some good shells there."

Bill's leathery face crinkled in a smile as he saw how eager they were. "Why, sure. Let the whole kit and kaboodle come."

"I'll pack a picnic lunch for us," Mrs. Merritt said.

It was agreed that they would start early the next day. *"After* breakfast," Judy was careful to add.

chapter 6

THE LOCKED DOOR

The next morning the sky was filled with puffy, grayish-white clouds. The water, too, where it met the sky was a dark grayish blue and only became lighter as it neared the shore.

True to his word, Bill rolled briskly into camp just as they were finishing breakfast. At least it seemed to Chuck that he rolled. With each step the old sailor swayed a little from side to side as if the sand were shifting under him.

"Ahoy," he called as soon as he was in shouting distance. "Are you ready for a voyage to the land of the cannibals?"

"You bet!" answered Chuck. Roger nodded eagerly.

Mrs. Merritt greeted her daughter's rescuer warmly. Judy and Henrietta ran to meet him. Henrietta licked the hand he petted her with and leaned against his knee.

In a few minutes the breakfast dishes were cleaned—first with sand, then with soap and water. And everybody was ready to go. Chuck grunted as he picked up the picnic basket his mother had loaded. "At least it'll be lighter coming back," he said.

Mrs. Merritt carried a couple of canvas bags made with special compartments for carrying artifacts. And from her shoulder hung the small but expensive camera that she used only to take pictures of things connected with her work.

Bill soon proved to be the best guide they could have picked. He knew the name of every plant and bird on Padre Island. He pointed out scuttling, tiny crabs and light-gray lizards darting between the strands of the purple-blossomed railroad vine.

41

And he showed them other small creatures they never would have seen if he hadn't been along.

Twice they came upon large flocks of birds that took to the air in quick retreat as Henrietta dashed, yapping, into their midst.

After they had been walking long enough to want a rest, Bill stopped and pointed with his hook. "This is the laguna, the quiet water that separates Padre from the mainland. Darn good fishing here, and it's where you come if you really want to see birds," he explained.

Chuck held Henrietta tight to keep her still while they watched in fascination. Hundreds of birds were fishing, swimming lazily, or dancing on the beach for the sheer joy of it.

At least fifty white pelicans beat their wings in rhythm on the water, chasing schools of tiny fish before them. From time to time they plunged their great beaks into the water to scoop up dozens of the frantic swimmers at a time.

They all laughed as they watched some of the odd looking pelicans begin their take-off runs. Beating their big wings, extending their huge beaks, and giving a series of hops, the awkward birds were finally airborne. Once in the air, though, they were graceful as butterflies.

"I wouldn't have missed this show for anything," declared Mrs. Merritt when Bill said they had better be getting on.

Bill set an easy pace so Henrietta's short legs could keep up. The going was faster now along the smooth edge of the laguna.

"I notice Henrietta doesn't seem to be limping since we left camp," observed Roger.

"That's because she's so brave," said Judy.

"You mean it's because she's been so busy she forgot to do it to get attention," snorted Chuck.

Another half hour of walking inland from the laguna brought the group to the site of the ancient Indian camp. Dr. Merritt was surprised at the size and location of the camp.

"Strange," she commented. "My map shows a Karankawa village farther to the south. But I don't see any indication on the map of this camp."

Bill chuckled. "Ain't surprising it's not on your map. Guess I'm the only one knew about it 'til today. Just happened to bump into it one day after the last big storm when I was cruising around these parts."

"You were lucky, Bill," said Dr. Merritt. "These old dunes are good at keeping secrets. Many scientists have spent a lot of time trying to find campsites they had once located."

"When they find them, why don't they mark them so they can come back to them?" asked Roger.

"They try to, but it's simply unbelievable what these shifting sands can cover and uncover—and in an amazingly short time," answered his aunt.

"Yeah," said Chuck. "Some people who buried their treasure here during the war thought they could find the spot again without any trouble because they remembered some marker, but then they never could locate it again."

"Let's get to digging," said Judy impatiently.

"Just a minute," said her mother. "Let me get some pictures first." With Bill's help she outlined the probable boundaries of the campsite, including within it a tall shell pile, or midden, and a strange circular spot with smooth, charred-looking rocks. She took pictures of the area from several angles.

"O.K., now we're ready to dig," said Dr. Merritt. "But remember, as soon as your digging tool touches anything, stop digging and call me."

They all began to dig eagerly but carefully in spots Bill pointed out to them as being worth trying.

"Have you removed any artifacts from here, Bill?" asked Roger.

"I don't think I read you, son." Bill scratched his red beard with his hook.

"Oh, I mean have you taken away any pieces of pottery, or jewelry, or arrowheads, or tomahawks, or the like?"

"Oh, sure," Bill nodded. "I've taken some of that stuff to my cabin. But there's plenty more here if you're willing to dig a little."

Just then Mrs. Merritt called out, "Look!" She pointed to a

piece of broken pottery. "This must have been part of a bowl of some kind. Let me get a picture and I'll finish uncovering it."

"Why, that's just a bit of clay from a broke pot, ma'am," said Bill. "I wouldn't trouble myself with that."

Dr. Merritt laughed. "Oh, Bill. To me it's a piece of treasure. See the design painted on it? That tells us a lot about the people who made it and used it. Fashions in pots changed over the years just as fashions in clothes do today, you know." Carefully she wrapped the potsherd in cotton batting and placed it in a pocket in one of the canvas bags.

"Mom, come look at these funny shells," said Chuck.

"Me, too," said Judy, hurrying over to watch as her mother with a tiny knife and a brush finished uncovering several shells with flecks of paint clinging to them.

"They might have been strung together to make a necklace," she said as she focused the camera to record their position on film.

Then Roger found a shell shaped like a knife and each of them found more potsherds, painted shells, and several arrowheads. Chuck found the head of a tomahawk, and Dr. Merritt dug up some stone beads that looked like little cigars with holes in each end.

Glancing up from his digging, Chuck noticed Barnacle Bill staring at the midden. As Chuck watched, Bill pulled something that looked like a piece of paper out of the top of the shell pile.

When he had read it, he muttered what sounded to Chuck like "Why, that little varmint!" Then he quickly stuck the piece of paper in his pocket.

At that moment Judy called her mother. "What are these lumps that look like tar?" she asked, pointing to some dark objects she had uncovered.

"That must be asphaltum. See the impressions on them; they were probably used to waterproof baskets. You must have found a spot where a basket used to be, Judy, but now all that's left is the natural asphalt coating. After I snap them, pick all the pieces up carefully and put them in the canvas bag."

When she had finished picking up the asphaltum, Judy announced, "I'm about to starve to death!" It was past twelve, and the others realized they were hungry, too. Soon they were seated in the shade of a dune devouring peanut butter and jelly sandwiches, cheese sandwiches, potato chips, oranges, and cookies.

As they ate, they talked about the Indians who had camped here. "They didn't have much likin' for staying in one place too long," said Bill. "They was always a-moving around, hunting better places to find fish and game."

"What do you suppose they used that place for?" asked Chuck, pointing to the pile of smooth, burned rocks.

"I reckon I know, but I don't want to frighten the little miss," answered Bill, nodding toward Judy.

"That's perfectly O.K. Henrietta and I were just going to look for shells." Judy strolled off toward the water, taking along a handful of cookies in case of a sudden attack of hunger. Henrietta followed reluctantly; she preferred to take a nap. But she knew she was supposed to keep track of the little girl.

"Now," said Chuck eagerly, "tell us about this place."

"Well, sir, it's enough to make your hair curl—to think of the things that happened right here on this very spot."

Sipping the root beer Mrs. Merritt had put in the thermos bottle, Bill glanced around the little group waiting to hear his story. He didn't often get a chance to be the center of interest, and he prepared to make the most of it.

"Imagine now," he began. "Dozens of them giant Indians—six-foot and over—all of 'em. Now just imagine how they look. They been on the warpath and got their faces painted—one side black and t'other side red. All the clothes they got on is just a little dinky apron.

"And the noise! It's enough to scare Davy Jones. They've got long whistles made out of canes. And drums made of turtles' shells with skin stretched over them. And rattles made out of gourds filled with pebbles. And there's the victim, poor fellow." Bill pointed with his hook toward the stones. "All tied, helpless as a fish out of water.

"Well, here are these yelling warriors a-dancing all around the poor fellow. In a while they gets themselves all worked up and about out of their minds."

Bill paused to look around slowly at his engrossed audience. At last he continued.

"Then's when they pulls out their knives and begins to whittle on him. The fire by them rocks is so's they can cook the pieces. And eat him right afore his own eyes, so to speak!"

Chuck and Roger stared at Bill with horrified attention. "I've read about that ritual; they called it the *Mitote,*" said Dr. Merritt.

" 'Course the victim didn't last too long," Bill added soothingly.

"What happened to the Karankawas?" asked Roger. "Why aren't there any today?"

"Well, sir," said Bill slowly, "to make a long story short, the Kronks didn't understand the ways of the white man, and the white man didn't understand the ways of the Kronks. And many a one of them died by guns and swords. When there was just a smidgen few left, they went to Mexico where they just kinda petered out after a few years."

"Here come Judy and Henrietta," said Mrs. Merritt. "If you all feel like digging some more, I need to finish my notes." Chuck knew his mother would write a careful description of each piece they had found and its exact location in the campsite.

After another hour of digging and turning up several more artifacts, they decided to start back. Bill had promised to show them some of the things he had found on Padre if they circled by his cabin.

At one point he stopped to show them a favorite area of the sand pirates who used to operate on the island some years before. As a sailor he had a deep hate for the illegal salvagers.

"Used to lure ships to shore by setting up false lights. Why, sometimes they'd tie a mast on the back of a burro and hang a lighted lantern on the top of it. Then those dirty rats would hobble the poor critter and drive it up and down the dunes.

The bobbin' light'd look just like the lights of ships in a harbor. Then those poor souls on that ship would be lured to their doom."

Roger looked at Bill seriously through his thick glasses. "But, didn't you say that some of your ancestors were pirates?"

"Twarn't the same thing. Not at all. Jean Lafitte and his men were honest-to-Gawd pirates. They came hellbent for leather a-roaring down on the enemy. You bet they did. They didn't go sneaking round with no lights tied to no burros. Sand pirates—bah!" With a vicious jab of his hook as though he was spearing one of the renegades, Bill dismissed the subject.

They spent a pleasant hour at Bill's shack. There was something to interest each of them in his collection of shells, Indian artifacts, pieces of ancient ships, and old coins. And along with each piece went an interesting story of its discovery.

Chuck was anxious to check on something he had only dimly noticed the other time they were in the building. As they had approached the outside from another angle this time, he was able to confirm his impression that there was a lean-to attached to the main room. Now he carefully scanned the back wall of the main room.

Sure enough, behind some fish netting that hung from the ceiling, there was a door. Billy Bones' cage hung just to the left of that door. While the others were absorbed in examining some dried fish specimens, Chuck casually walked over to the cage.

Pretending to talk to the bird who persisted in requesting "a little drink," Chuck laid his hand on the doorknob and turned it. The door was locked.

Glancing at the others to make sure their backs were still turned, he bent and put his eye to the old-fashioned keyhole. Then he almost fell over backwards.

There on the other side of the keyhole was another eye— looking at him! Before he could recover from his surprise, it was gone. There was a slight scurrying sound on the other side of the door. Then complete silence.

It all happened so fast, Chuck wondered for a second if he

had imagined that he had seen an eye and heard a noise. But he knew he hadn't. He moved toward the others who were examining a huge starfish. They were obviously unaware of what had happened to him.

When they started back to camp a few minutes later, Barnacle Bill walked a little way with them. As he turned to leave them, he squinted at the sky.

"Don't like the looks of them clouds," he said. Chuck noticed that while they were in Bill's shack, the sky had become filled with layers and layers of large, dark puffs of clouds. "Better watch out; we may have some weather soon," warned the old sailor as he left them.

Chuck signaled to Roger to let Mrs. Merritt and Judy walk on ahead. Then he told him about what he had seen and heard back in the cabin.

"A locked door could mean a lot of things," said Roger thoughtfully. "He might be keeping some valuable treasure in there. Or some kind of animal. Maybe that was what you saw. The eye of an animal."

"I don't think so." Chuck shook his head. "It sure looked like a human eye."

Chuck pushed the lock of hair out of his eyes. "I saw something else strange at the Indian camp today. Just before we ate lunch."

"*You* did?" Roger stopped walking to stare at Chuck. "I thought I saw something odd, too. But I wasn't sure. What was it you saw?"

"Well, I saw Barnacle Bill pull some kind of folded paper out of a big shell pile. And it sounded like he said something about 'a little varmint' when he read it."

"I didn't see that. But I did notice that Bill put half a sandwich and some cookies in his pocket when he thought no one was looking. I thought he was stocking up for a snack later like Judy does. But now I wonder."

"Yeah, me, too." As the two boys began to catch up with the rest of the family, Chuck watched his mother's back.

"Wish we could ask Mom about it. She's good at figuring out

things. But she doesn't like for me to stick my nose in other people's business. And I *know* what she'd say about peeking through the keyhole!"

Roger laughed. "So do I! We'll just have to keep our eyes and ears open for more clues."

"Right!" Chuck agreed. "There've got to be some answers for the strange things that have happened since we came to Padre!"

chapter 7

A STORMY DAY

That night Chuck slept restlessly. Tall, painted Indians danced in his dreams. Once he thought he was on a ship about to run aground while grinning sand pirates waited on shore with a burro that had a lantern tied to its back. Just as the schooner was about to pile up on the sandy shore he awoke.

He sat up trying to figure out what had disturbed him. Then he realized it was the wind. He was used to the constant breeze that blew on the island, but this wind was different. It came in strong gusts, followed by periods of calm in which there was no breeze at all.

Chuck peered through the tent opening at the sky. The heavy, hanging clouds seemed to be doing a kind of dance high over his head, and the light that came through them was an unnatural greenish-yellow color.

For a long time Chuck lay awake watching the clouds. He was trying to decide whether to get up or go back to sleep when he saw his mother and Henrietta walk briskly past the opening. His mother had a package in her arms.

He jumped up and pulled on his jeans and T-shirt. Mrs. Merritt looked up from her breakfast preparations and smiled as he came out of the tent. "Good morning, Chuck."

"Hi, Mom. Where've you and Hen been already?"

"We walked to the McClines to get some milk and fresh doughnuts. I heard a weather report while we were there. We may be in for some heavy rain."

"Yeah, I've been watching those funny clouds. Bill knew

what he was talking about yesterday."

"Yes, you can depend on an old sailor to know his weather signs. I'm just wondering if we ought to pack up and go to visit Aunt Mabel and Uncle John early."

"Oh, no, we can't leave yet," wailed Judy, who had just walked up. "My shell collection is incomplete."

"Roger and I have some unfinished business, too," said Chuck. "Our treasure hunting—and uh—other things."

Looking at their unhappy faces, Dr. Merritt said, "Well, let's have breakfast and listen to the car radio to catch the weather report. Then we can decide what to do."

With the help of Henrietta, Chuck routed Roger out of his sleeping bag, and they were soon eating cereal with bananas, doughnuts, and milk.

The weather announcer predicted heavy rain for the Padre Island and Corpus Christi area with winds gusting up to forty miles per hour.

"Will it be a hurricane?" asked Judy.

"No," Roger answered, "the winds have to be at least seventy-five miles per hour for a storm to be a hurricane."

"Boy, that would be exciting—to be on an island during a hurricane," said Chuck.

"A little too exciting, Chuck," said Dr. Merritt. "The worst danger on a coastal island is tidal water. Huge waves might wash over the island and sweep us all far out into the Gulf."

"Wow!" said Chuck.

"Oh," said Judy.

"Don't worry," said Dr. Merritt. "I assure you if a hurricane was coming anywhere near Padre, there wouldn't be any question about leaving the island. But as it is—I don't know—if you all really want to stay . . ."

"We do," the three children answered her in chorus.

"All right, then. But we'll need to make things shipshape in case the rain is heavy and the winds do get strong."

Everyone worked hard to get the campsite in shape to weather the rainstorm. Chuck and Roger made sure that all the stakes and ties on the tents were secured. The boys' smaller tent was closed completely and the sides weighted down with heavy pieces of driftwood after the cots had been moved into the larger tent. The folding table, chairs, food and water supplies were also brought into the large tent. Mrs. Merritt moved the car to the side of the tent facing the water to act as a windbreak.

As they worked, Chuck noticed that one minute everything seemed hot and still, and the next the wind was blowing in gusts. Excited by the unusual atmosphere and all the activity, Henrietta ran from one to the other and managed to get in everybody's way.

"Can you boys rig up an indoor bathroom, in case this lasts awhile?" asked Mrs. Merritt.

"Sure, Mom," said Chuck. With Roger's help he stretched a clothesline over the corner of the tent and hung a blanket behind the improvised curtain.

"There you are, the latest in plumbing."

Roger laughed. "Remind me not to hire you to do my plumbing!"

As the morning wore on the cloud cover grew blacker and thicker. From time to time streaks of lightning darted out of it. The breakers in the Gulf were a strange, ugly, yellow-gray color.

"It doesn't seem very friendly here anymore," said Judy.

"Yeah," agreed Chuck, and Roger nodded.

"O.K., remember you all wanted to stay," Dr. Merritt reminded them, "so let's not have any long faces. We'll retire to our snug tent and 'ride it out' as Bill would say."

Just then they heard the first rumble of thunder. Henrietta growled in reply, and everyone laughed. Big drops of rain began to splat around them and after a hurried check of the campsite, they all went into the big tent.

By the time they had fixed and eaten a sandwich lunch, it was raining so hard they could only see a few feet through the front opening. The lightning flashed, and the thunder cracked loudly every few minutes now.

Mrs. Merritt lit a lantern, and the inside of the tent seemed more cheerful. For several hours the three children sat cross-legged on two cots playing card games and Chinese checkers. Henrietta lay curled up at the end of one cot growling low in her throat at the thunder every so often.

When they tired of their games, Mrs. Merritt suggested they read aloud from one of their family reading books. "What would you like?" she asked. "I packed *The Hobbit, Wind in the Willows,* and *The Peterkin Papers.*"

"*The Hobbit!*" said Chuck.

"*Wind in the Willows!*" said Judy.

"Well, what do you say, Roger?" asked his aunt.

Roger looked serious and thought for a minute. "Both of those are interesting, and *The Peterkin Papers* has some funny stories. Could we read a little from all three?"

"That's a very good idea," said Judy.

"O.K. by me," said Chuck.

"All right," said Mrs. Merritt. "I'll read first from *The Wind in the Willows.* Then you can take turns reading from the others while I get supper ready."

The lightning and thunder had died down, but the rain continued to drum on the canvas, and the wind still howled. "It sounds like a giant is trying to huff and puff our tent down!" said Judy.

Mrs. Merritt smiled at her daughter. "Shall I read your favorite chapter, Judy, about the little lost otter child?"

"Yes," said Judy, "it always makes me feel safe when Rat and Mole find him and take him home to his father." So Mrs. Merritt read the chapter called "The Piper at the Gates of Dawn." When she finished everyone sat quietly for a few minutes without saying anything.

Then Mrs. Merritt got up. "Who's next?"

"I could read the part in *The Hobbit* where Bilbo and the Gollum ask riddles," Chuck offered. Judy and Roger agreed. And after that Roger read the chapter in *The Peterkin Papers* about Elizabeth Eliza's piano, which they all thought was funny.

When Roger had finished reading, Mrs. Merritt gave them

paper plates with vienna sausages, cheese slices, sliced tomatoes, bread and butter, and cookies. They each had paper cups with milk. "We're just having cold food tonight," explained Mrs. Merritt, "because I don't think it would be a good idea to light the portable stove in here with it all closed up."

"At least it'll be easy to clean up," said Chuck.

"It's too early to go to bed," said Judy when they had finished eating. "What can we do now?"

"We could play '20 Questions,'" suggested Roger.

"Good idea," said Mrs. Merritt.

After several rounds they began to run out of ideas of things to ask about, and Judy suggested they tell stories—but "not ghost stories."

Mrs. Merritt, who knew a lot about mythology, told them stories about Hercules, the strong man, and Medusa, the snake-haired woman. Roger and Chuck told some of the myths they had studied in school.

"Goodness," exclaimed Mrs. Merritt, "do you all know it's almost ten o'clock? We'd better get ourselves to bed."

Long after the others were asleep, Chuck lay awake listening to the steady pounding of the rain. He thought about the things that had happened in the last five days since they arrived on Padre. He wondered what the—whatever it was that had been acting so mysteriously since their arrival—was doing in the rainstorm.

He rolled over and accidentally kicked Henrietta, who was sleeping at the end of his cot. She muttered a protest. "Sorry, old girl," he whispered.

"I can't keep calling it the 'whatever it is,'" he thought. "I know. It's been acting so spooky, I'll call it 'The Ghost.' Yeah, 'The Ghost of Padre Island'. And before we leave here, Mr. Ghost, I'll know who you *really* are or my name's not Charles William Merritt!"

chapter 8

PIRATE SHIP

Sometime during the night the rain stopped. When Chuck woke up, the sun was shining brightly. His mother, Judy, and Henrietta were out of the tent, and he smelled bacon cooking. Roger still lay snuggled in his sleeping bag.

Judy poked her head in the tent opening. "Come on, you lazies. Breakfast is ready, and Henrietta and I have been exploring, and the beach is in a terrible mess."

When Chuck and Roger came out of the tent they saw that Judy was right. The wind-driven waves had piled driftwood, seaweed, and other debris in jumbled heaps all up and down the beach as far as they could see.

"That storm was some litterbug!" said Chuck.

"I've already found three sea beans," said Judy, showing them the large, brown beans. "And there are some gorgeous jellyfish on the beach. But we have to be careful not to let Henrietta touch them."

"I know," said Chuck. He remembered another time at the beach when he had seen a man in great pain from being stung by a jellyfish.

After they had eaten, they all went to work cleaning out the area around their camp. The morning was gone by the time they had cleared the area all the way to the water and set up the camp furniture and supplies in their places again.

When they finished lunch Dr. Merritt said, "I think I'll take a nap; I woke up early this morning."

"Roger and I were talking about going to Bill's to see if the

56

storm did any damage to his cabin," said Chuck.

"Me, too," said Judy.

"That's a good idea, boys, do you mind if Judy goes along?"

"I guess not," said Chuck.

Henrietta, of course, didn't wait to be asked.

The route to the cabin looked strange. Often they had to pick their way around piles of debris and stacks of driftwood. They had to keep a close watch on Henrietta, who was continually sniffing the skeletons of dead fish or getting dangerously close to jellyfish.

Bill's cabin looked the same as it always did. The rope coils were in front of it, and the nets were strung along the side. If any damage had been done to the roof or windows, it had already been repaired.

The front door was closed but not locked. After knocking a couple of times and getting no answer, Chuck opened the door a crack and called, "Anybody home? Bill, are you there?"

This time he got an answer. "Hello. Hello. Come in, come in. How about a little rum?" It was only Mr. Bones, offering his usual greeting.

After walking around the building and calling a number of times, they were sure Bill was not in the neighborhood. Chuck was tempted to try the lean-to door, but decided he'd better not. He didn't want to have to explain to Judy how he knew about the locked door.

"Well," said Roger. "I guess we'll have to come back in the morning and try to catch Bill at home."

"Let's go back a different way," suggested Chuck. He pointed away from the beach. "If we walk back there, we won't have to worry so much about keeping Hen away from dead fish and jellyfish."

A short way along their detour route, they made an exciting find. The three children caught sight of it at the same time and called out together, "Look, a ship!"

"It looks awfully old," said Chuck.

"It looks like the pictures of old sailing schooners," said Roger. He began to pace off the length. "Yep, sixty-five feet.

That's just about right."

"Here are some funny square nails," said Chuck. "And a sheet of glass, not even broken."

"Probably the material it was wrapped in rotted away," said Roger.

The ribs of the ship were of heavy cedar. At one end was the carved figurehead of a woman with bits of paint still clinging to it.

"Maybe this ship got lost in a big storm," said Judy.

"Say, it might have been a treasure ship," said Chuck.

"I doubt it, Chuck," said Roger. "Probably most of the ships washed ashore on Padre by storms just carried ordinary supplies, you know."

"Yeah," sighed Chuck, kicking at some rotted remains of bales of merchandise. "But you know what I just thought?" Judy and Roger looked at him questioningly.

"Don't you think Barnacle Bill would have known about this ship? It's not far from his cabin. The other day when he brought us back from the Indian campsite we must have passed close by here, and he could have shown this to us."

"But he didn't." Roger shook his head slowly.

"So that's another odd thing," said Chuck. "Well, anyway, it would be a great place to play pirates and Spaniards."

"You mean real pirates, not sand pirates," said Roger.

"Right," said Chuck, grinning. "Let's try it."

The three took turns being the Spaniards and the attacking pirates. The Spaniard pretended to sail the ship in the choppy waters of the Gulf. When the pirates challenged him to "stand and deliver," the defender pulled out his driftwood sword, and a duel was fought.

The duels were always won by the pirate, who then made the Spaniard walk the plank. Of course, the role of the plank walker was the favorite one. Roger and Chuck had fixed a board to extend over the imaginary deck of the ship and on out over a small dune.

Judy's bandanna was used to blindfold the victim, whose hands were tied behind him with a piece of drift rope. He fell

into the soft dune with a satisfying thud and had to scramble up in a hurry to keep Henrietta from rushing over to lick his face to revive him.

At last they tired of the game and returned to camp. The sleeping was fine that night in the cool, clear air.

After an early breakfast, the whole family again went to visit Bill. But again they found the cabin empty except for Mr. Bones.

As they were standing uncertainly in front of the door, Chuck noticed Henrietta with her nose in the sand following a scent. She seemed to be moving along a line of shells. After examining the row of shells closely, Chuck called to the others, "Hey, look at this. It's a shell trail. I'm certain it wasn't here yesterday."

The others agreed that the shells appeared to be carefully laid out to form a line leading away from the cabin.

"Let's follow it and see where it leads," cried Judy. Henrietta had already decided to do just that, and the others set out after her.

For almost half an hour they climbed up, down, and around dunes. There were a number of detours around clumps of storm-piled rubbish, but always the trail remained clearly marked.

Chuck was the only one who could keep up with Henrietta when she was on a hot trail. Soon the two of them got to be a long way ahead of the others.

Coming around a large dune Chuck saw something in the sand next to a large piece of driftwood. He stopped abruptly.

It was the figure of a man, and it was lying very, very still. Chuck's throat felt tight. It looked like a dead man!

chapter 9

A TREASURE MAP

"Wait, Henrietta!" Chuck tried to grab the excited dog. But she went running straight to the still figure, and when she reached it she sat down and started whimpering.

Chuck walked forward slowly until he could see over the piece of driftwood. Then he raced the last few steps. The man lying in the sand was Barnacle Bill!

Now that he was closer Chuck could see that the old sailor's chest was moving—at least he was breathing. But he didn't respond when Chuck called his name. He appeared to be unconscious.

In a few minutes the others joined Chuck. Dr. Merritt exclaimed, "Look! Someone has already given him first aid. He must have been bitten by a snake."

Sure enough, Bill's swollen ankle was propped up on a piece of driftwood. There was a small x-shaped cut over the fang marks and a bandage tied above the cut. A blanket had been placed under his head for a pillow.

"It must have been the same person who made the shell trail to lead us here!" said Roger.

Suddenly Judy pointed. "Look at Henrietta!" The short-legged dog was tugging and pulling with all her might. She had something long and dark in her mouth that she was trying to bring over to them.

Chuck ran over to investigate. "It's a dead rattlesnake," he called. "Its head is smashed in."

"Whoever took care of Bill must have killed the snake, too," said Roger.

It was quickly decided that Dr. Merritt would go back to camp to get the car while the others stayed with Bill. It would be impossible to drive through the soft sand and dunes to the spot where they found him. He would have to be carried to the station wagon, so Roger and Chuck began to make an emergency stretcher out of the blanket and some driftwood pieces.

"Leave that nasty, old thing alone," said Judy, pulling Henrietta away from the snake. When he and Roger had finished the stretcher, Chuck came over to cut the rattles—it was a large snake with eight rattles—to add to what Judy called his collection of "awfuls." The collection included such things as a tarantula and a preserved baby octopus.

In a short time, Dr. Merritt was back to help them carry Bill down to the car. She had driven it as far as she dared off the hardpacked sand road along the beach.

With the four of them helping and Henrietta leading the procession, they soon had their patient stretched out on the pillows and blankets that Dr. Merritt had thrown in the back of the station wagon. Then she left for the hospital in Corpus Christi, and the others headed back to camp.

No one was hungry for lunch, and none of their games seemed interesting. Chuck suggested fishing or shell hunting, but nobody felt like doing either one.

Henrietta lay with her head between her outstretched front paws rolling her sad eyes up at them as if she shared their mood.

Finally Judy blurted out what was bothering all of them. "Wh-what if Barnacle Bill dies? What if we didn't find him in time for the doctors to save him?" She burst into tears.

Chuck and Roger looked at each other helplessly. Chuck said, "Don't cry, Judy, we've just got to hope for the best."

Roger added, "It was sure lucky that someone gave him first aid, and now he's getting real medical help."

The gloomy afternoon finally wore away. It was suppertime but nobody mentioned eating. Then Henrietta jumped up and began barking; the station wagon was driving up.

They bombarded Dr. Merritt with questions before she could open her mouth.

"Wait a minute. Wait a minute." She held up her hand. "How can I tell you anything if you don't let me talk?" Then she grinned. "The news is good. I stayed until the doctors felt sure. Bill is resting comfortably and will be able to return home in a few days."

Chuck let out a loud cheer, and Roger joined in. Judy hugged her mother. And Henrietta tried to jump up on everyone.

"How did Bill say it happened?" asked Roger

"I didn't bother him with questions," answered Dr. Merritt. "After he became conscious and the doctor told me he'd be all right, I just told him we'd be back to see him and left."

Suddenly everyone was ravenous. "Let's have a wiener roast!" said Chuck. Mrs. Merritt agreed and soon the boys were building a driftwood fire and sharpening sticks.

Judy laid out graham crackers, chocolate bars, and marshmallows to make s'mores for dessert. It was a dish she liked to prepare, and it was a popular one with the rest of the family.

When no one could eat another bite, Mrs. Merritt suggested a moonlight wade. Soon they were all splashing in the surf. The huge moon seemed to hang just over the water. In the distance the lights of the shrimp boats and oil derricks glittered.

Henrietta romped in the waves like a puppy, splashing all of them. Judy squealed as tiny fish and pieces of seaweed rubbed against her feet and ankles making her think that a crab might be nibbling at them.

At last they returned to their tents for a good sleep after a long, anxious day. As the others were preparing for bed, Judy let out an anguished wail. "Who took my dessert?"

"Whatever do you mean?" asked her mother in surprise.

"I had saved two s'mores to eat before I went to bed. I wrapped them in foil and put them right there behind the paper towels. And now they're gone!" Judy looked accusingly at her brother and Roger.

"I didn't take them!" said Chuck indignantly.

"Neither did I," said Roger. "After all I ate at supper I couldn't stuff in another mouthful."

"Well, Judy, you certainly didn't need the extra dessert," said Dr. Merritt, "but it is strange that they disappeared."

"Let's look and see if anything else is missing," suggested Chuck.

"Good idea," said Dr. Merritt. After a careful check of their belongings, they all reported that nothing seemed to be missing.

"Wait a minute," said Mrs. Merritt. She made a quick inspection of the cooking area. "There is something. Those two leftover hot dogs and buns are gone, too."

They searched the area for footprints, but could find none in the soft sand. Since no amount of talking could solve the puzzle of the hungry thief, the tired campers trailed off one by one to bed.

Chuck lay awake for a long time trying to think of some logical answer to the mystery. But he could come up with no explanation that made sense.

The next morning he was up before the others, determined to hunt for clues that they might have overlooked in the dark.

An hour of painstaking searching of the area around the camp left him as puzzled as ever. The blank sand seemed to mock his efforts to force it to yield its secrets to him.

After breakfast the children decided to visit their pirate ship. They had been playing on it for a few minutes when Roger picked up an old, rusty can that was lying in what would have been about the middle of the deck if the skeleton ship had had a deck.

"Wonder how this got here. It wasn't here when we found the ship day before yesterday," he remarked.

He was about to toss it away when Judy, looking over his shoulder, said, "Wait. I think there's a piece of paper in it."

Roger pulled out the dirty piece of folded paper. Opening it he said, "It's only somebody's directions for how to get somewhere."

"Hold on," said Chuck. He had taken the map and was looking at it closely. Pointing to a spot in the lower left hand corner
he showed Roger. "What does it say right under the large 'X'?"

"The printing's so poor it's hard to tell." Roger brought the
paper closer to his glasses and spelled out B-E-R-R-I-E-D
T-R-A-Y-S-H-O-R. He laughed. "The spelling's worse than
the writing!"

"It might mean something," argued Chuck. "Pirates might
not be able to spell very well. I bet they didn't spend much time
in school!"

"Aw, Chuck, be reasonable. Look at the paper," Roger held it
up to the light. "It's just like the tablet paper that's used by
every kid in elementary school. Besides, you can see it's not
very old even if it is dirty from being in that old can."

"Just the same I think we ought to try to figure it out," said
Chuck stubbornly. "Somebody had to put it there. And they
must have intended for us to find it."

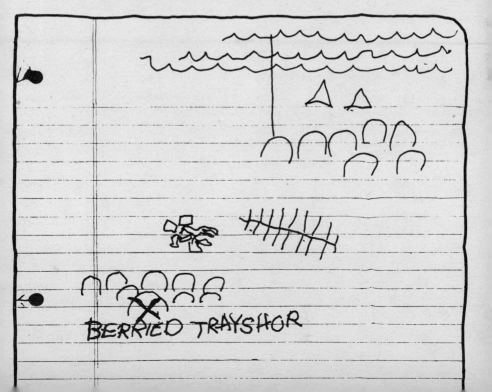

"That's right," said Judy. "This is our ship. So the map must be for us."

"Well, sure," said Roger. "Let's try to figure it out, but just don't expect it to lead us to any pirate treasure."

He spread the paper out on the sand, and the three heads bent over it.

After a minute, Roger said, "That's probably water there at the top, but the rest doesn't make any sense to me."

Suddenly Chuck felt as though someone had turned on a light inside his head. "I think I understand it. We can check it out after lunch. Maybe Mom will want to come with us."

When they showed Mrs. Merritt the map she agreed with Roger that the paper looked quite modern. "It may be someone's idea of a joke. Of course, you can try to follow it if you want to, but I think I'll stay here and finish labeling these artifacts we got from the Indian campsite."

As the treasure hunters set out after lunch, she smiled at them. "Don't be disappointed if you don't find anything. I'm afraid in real life people just don't go around burying valuable objects and leaving maps in tin cans for anyone to find."

When they were a little way from camp, Chuck pulled out the map. "Here's what I figure." He laid his finger on the wavy lines. "That's the Gulf, and those two triangles are our tents. And the horseshoe shapes around them are dunes. O.K.?"

Roger's dark head and Judy's blond one nodded in agreement. Henrietta wagged her tail as if she understood also.

"Then," Chuck continued, "that tall, skinny thing is the old flag pole near our camp. And the thing that looks like a fish skeleton is our pirate ship."

"Sure," said Roger, "now I see it. But what's that bunch of funny looking shapes beyond that?"

"I don't know," admitted Chuck. "Haven't gotten that far yet. Let's go to the ship and start from there, and maybe we can figure the rest of it out."

In a few minutes they had arrived at the ship's skeleton. Chuck and Roger studied the map again.

"Too bad our map maker didn't know you're supposed to say

so many paces in such and such a direction," said Roger.

"Well, anyway, it looks as though we should continue to walk away from the water," said Chuck. "Let's spread out a little and sing out if you see anything that looks like the drawing."

For several minutes they walked along studying the landscape intently. Then Roger called out, "Come here. What do you think about that?" He pointed to a large pile of driftwood, boards, and crates that were piled up against the low dune.

Chuck whistled. "I think that's it, Rog. And if these horseshoe shapes are dunes, we're almost there. Here are a batch of small dunes. And that one sticking up way over there with the cactus plant on its side looks like the one where the 'X' is!"

Slipping and sliding, the three raced across the low dunes with Henrietta barking alongside them. Arriving at the foot of the tall dune, they stopped for a minute puzzled. There was not the slightest sign that the rippled sand had ever been disturbed.

"Where shall we start?" asked Roger.

"Guess it doesn't matter," answered Chuck. "Let's each begin digging close to the base of the dune and work our way all around it. Then we can branch out and continue to work in circles around it—until something turns up," he added hopefully.

Roger and Chuck set to work with their hand shovels and Judy with a garden trowel. Henrietta had only her paws and nose, but she joined in the digging eagerly.

It was fairly easy digging. A few inches under the white sand they discovered layers of black sand. They decided to dig about a foot down each time and then move on to a new spot.

When they had been digging for about half an hour and had worked their way about a third of the way around the dune, Roger called out, "Hey, I've hit something!"

Chuck and Judy rushed to help uncover the object Roger's shovel was clanking against. The sand sifted back into the holes as fast as Roger threw it out, as though it didn't want them to discover what it held.

At last the object was freed of sand. Roger picked it up eager-ly. "Why, it's only an old rock!" he said in disgust, flinging it aside.

Silently the trio returned to digging. After another un-rewarding fifteen minutes, Chuck said, "Let's take a break."

They were all glad to sit in the shade of the dune, taking cool drinks from the canteen.

As they rested Chuck idly turned over the round, flat rock that Roger had dug up. Suddenly he sat upright. "This rock has writing on it!" he exclaimed.

chapter 10

BERRIED TRAYSHOR

Roger and Judy stared at Chuck as he slowly spelled out the wobbly letters crudely carved into the surface of the rock.

"It says, 'Dig Deeper,' " he announced dramatically.

"It's the rock that Jean Lafitte and his pirates buried their treasure under!" Judy clapped her hands in excitement.

"No," Roger shook his head. "It couldn't be. It says in the *Guide* that that rock was very large—probably an old millstone. This little old rock is not much bigger than my two hands put together."

"Well, anyway, somebody carved the words on it and put it there for us to find by using the treasure map. So let's do what it says!" Chuck grabbed up his shovel; then he stopped. "Where did you find the rock, Roger?"

"Gosh, I don't know," said Roger, shaking his head. The sand holes they had dug were almost all filled in. He stared at the dune intently. Then he pointed at the cactus plant.

"I remember now! I was digging almost right under that cactus when I hit it."

Frantically the three of them began to make the sand fly in the area below the cactus. Before long Roger called, "I've hit something again. This must be it!"

Throwing down their tools, the trio dug furiously with their hands until they had uncovered what appeared to be the top of a flat metal box. Carefully they scooped it out of the sand.

It was a gray box about eighteen inches square and about ten inches deep. It seemed to be the kind of box that a ship might carry to hold valuable papers. It had no lock, being fastened only with simple snap-lock fasteners.

For a minute the three sat in stunned silence as if they didn't really believe what they saw. Then Judy cried, "Open it! Open it!"

Chuck pushed back the locks on each side and pulled open the lid. Inside, carefully wrapped in canvas and tied with stout cord, were five packages of different sizes. Slipped under the cord of each package was a folded piece of paper of the same kind that the map had been drawn on.

Roger carefully drew one of the pieces of paper out from under the twine that held it in place. "It's a picture!" He held it out for them to see.

"It looks like a little girl with pigtails!" said Chuck. Even though the drawing was rough, it was plain that it was intended to represent a small girl with her hair in pigtails.

"Like me," said Judy wonderingly.

Chuck withdrew another of the folded pieces of paper. "This one is a boy with black hair wearing glasses—like you, Rog!"

"And this one is a lady with short curly hair," said Judy carefully examining the paper from a third package.

"Wait a minute. Let's not get them mixed up. Don't you see what they mean? Each package must be intended for the person whose picture is on it." Chuck and Judy stared at Roger.

Then Chuck nodded. "Sure. The lady must be Mom. And one of them is for each of us. But who is the fifth one for?"

"Let's see," said Roger. "First put each picture back on top of the package it came from. Now let's look at the other two."

One was a rough drawing of a boy with a lock of hair falling over one eye—Chuck had to laugh at this picture of himself.

The last picture had evidently caused the artist the most trouble. It was of a black dog with short bowed legs and a long nose. The large sad eyes and the long tail had been erased and redrawn several times.

"He took more trouble with Henrietta's picture than he did with anyone else's," Roger commented.

"But mine is the biggest package. Let's open them now!" said Judy impatiently.

"O.K. One at a time—like Christmas," said Chuck.

Judy struggled to untie the knots that fastened the canvas around her package. When he saw she was about to use her teeth, Chuck said, "Wait, Judy," and pulled out his pocket knife and cut the knots for her.

Folding back the canvas, she uncovered a beautiful spiral shell with tints of pink blending into the white. And next to it was a blue-green Japanese fishing ball.

"Oh-h-h," breathed Judy, "it's the most gorgeous shell I've ever seen. And I have a fishing ball of my very own now!"

"O.K., Rog, now you," said Chuck.

Roger cut through the knots neatly on his package and unwrapped it to reveal six excellent Indian arrowheads.

"They're in perfect condition. And look how sharp the edges are on them. Aren't they neat?" Roger waved his hand vaguely toward the dunes. "Thank you, Mr. Ghost, whoever you are!"

Chuck's hands shook a little from excitement as he unwrapped his package. It contained two very old looking coins that Roger identified tentatively in the *Guide* as four-real pieces. "Gosh," Chuck whispered as he turned the coins over in his palm.

"Now you have the treasure you've been hunting for ever since we got here," said Judy.

"Yeah," said Chuck in a bewildered voice, "but how in the world could anyone have known just the right thing to pick out for each of us?"

"We haven't opened Henrietta's package. Let's see what he picked out for her," said Judy.

Chuck cut the knots on the fourth package. Inside was a ball—not a bought ball, but a carefully handmade one. Strong twine was wrapped round and round until it made a ball just the right size for Henrietta to catch in her mouth.

"It took some work to make that," said Roger.

"I think the ghost likes Henrietta best," said Judy.

That evening after Dr. Merritt unwrapped her package, she

sat turning over in her hands the bits of pottery and painted shells that had been in it. "This is truly a mystery. I haven't found any potsherds as nice as these. And the shells are in better condition than any I've come across so far."

"Look, Mom, there's something else," Judy pointed.

Mrs. Merritt shook the piece of canvas, and into her lap fell a brooch made of yellow gold and clustered with tiny pearls.

"My goodness! This looks like a very old piece of Spanish jewelry," she exclaimed.

"It was probably on one of the Spanish ships that was wrecked on Padre," said Chuck.

Mrs. Merritt shook her head in wonder. "If this is in payment for the food our friendly ghost has helped himself to, I am greatly overpaid."

"But who on earth—or on Padre Island—knows us well enough to pick out just the right thing for all of us?" said Roger.

"The only ones who know us here are the McClines and Barnacle Bill," said Chuck.

"And he's been in the hospital since yesterday," said Judy. "Anyway, there's nothing mysterious about him."

"Don't be too sure about that," said Chuck before he thought. His mother and Judy looked at him curiously. Roger, of course, understood what he meant.

"What do you mean, Chuck?" asked his mother.

With a slight shrug of his shoulders Chuck indicated to Roger that since he had gone this far, they might as well tell all they knew.

He told them first about the note he had seen Bill remove from the shell midden the day they went on the expedition to the Indian camp.

"I thought Bill said he was the only one that knew about that camp," said Dr. Merritt.

"He did," said Chuck. "But he didn't seem surprised to find the note there."

Roger told of seeing the old sailor put the extra food into his pockets.

Then Chuck reluctantly told about the locked door of the

lean-to. As he had expected, his mother didn't approve of his investigation of the door.

"Quite likely he locks it because he keeps his more valuable possessions in there," she said. "He may have found some fairly valuable treasure in his years of beachcombing."

"Well," said Chuck, "don't forget how angry he was that first day when we wandered into his cabin. And he always seems to want to know in advance when we're coming to visit him."

"People who live isolated lives often are overprotective of their privacy," answered Dr. Merritt. "And sometimes they become a little eccentric in their behavior."

"What does 'ex-centric' mean?" demanded Judy.

"It means doing things that are a little odd—like squirreling away food to eat between meals." She pulled one of Judy's pigtails. "Do you know anyone in this family who is a little eccentric?"

"I don't know what you're talking about," said Judy with dignity. The others laughed.

"Well, anyway, even if Bill has some odd habits, it seems he can't have been the one who has given us the treasures." Mrs. Merritt shivered a little as the long, drawn-out wail of a coyote echoed over the dunes.

"It makes me feel a little uncomfortable to know that someone has been watching us closely enough to know so much about our tastes."

For a long time after they had crawled into their sleeping bags Chuck and Roger talked over the day's events. Chuck's last thought before he fell asleep was, "We've only got a few more days on Padre left. I've just got to solve this mystery before we leave here—or bust!"

chapter 11

SETTING A TRAP

In the morning as they were eating breakfast, Mrs. Merritt and Judy announced their plans for the day. They wanted to go into Corpus Christi to shop at a big supermarket for groceries that the little store on Padre didn't carry.

"And we want to see how Uncle John and Aunt Mabel are getting on. You boys can spend the day there if you want to," said Mrs. Merritt.

"And we're going to visit Bill at the hospital," added Judy. "I've already picked some flowers to take him." She held up a bunch of slightly wilted primroses and morning glories wrapped in a damp paper towel.

Chuck made a face. "Girls! Men don't want old droopy flowers."

Mrs. Merritt smiled at her daughter. "I'm sure he'll appreciate the fact that you care about him and went to the trouble to pick the flowers." She looked thoughtfully at the bouquet. "I wouldn't be surprised if it wasn't the first time in his life that anyone ever gave him flowers."

Chuck and Roger had been exchanging eye signals. Chuck spoke to his mother. "Can't Roger and I stay here? We only have a few days left, and we don't want to miss any more time on Padre."

"Well, I know you can take care of yourselves, but . . ." Mrs. Merritt began.

"We promise not to do anything dangerous," said Chuck. "We'll go to the Indian camp and see if the storm changed anything there, if you want us to."

"All right," said Mrs. Merritt. "But it will be after dark when we get back. Shall I leave you something fixed for supper?"

"No," said Chuck. "We'll catch our own dinner. O.K., Rog?"

"You bet," said Roger. The surf had been so rough after the storm that they hadn't been able to do any fishing.

The day passed pleasantly. In the morning they hiked along the laguna to the Indian campsite following the landmarks Bill had shown them. The area showed little effects from the winds and waves as it was far removed from the beach.

After lunch and a rest they waded out into the surf past the first line of sand bars to fish. The water was calm again and they could see fish making silver arcs as they leaped into the air.

"Fish are jumping today," said Roger.

"Yeah, we better jump too it we want to eat tonight," said Chuck. "The gulls know where the fishing is best. Let's try over there where they're circling."

The fish were hungry, too. In fact the fishing was so good they could afford to be choosy. They threw back the smaller fish until they got exactly the sizes they wanted. In a short time they each had two good-sized redfish.

"This is more than enough for dinner and breakfast. And we can't store any more than that, so I guess we'd better quit," said Chuck.

Roger scaled and cleaned the fish while Chuck stirred up some skillet cornbread as his dad had taught him to do when they used to go on fishing trips together.

Then he rolled the fish in cornmeal and fried them to a golden brown. Roger sighed with contentment. "I didn't know fish could taste so good!"

"Yeah," Chuck said. "Dad used to say fish always tastes best when it's eaten in sight of the water it was caught in."

After they had eaten all they could and given Henrietta all she wanted, Chuck said, "Rog, I've got an idea I'll tell you about while we clean up."

A few minutes later as he scoured out the frying pan Roger

said, "O.K., what's the deal?"

"I've been trying to think of a way to catch the ghost." As he talked Chuck was wrapping up a leftover piece of fish and a slice of cornbread in foil. "Since this is such a hungry ghost, why not bait a trap with food? And since he left a message for us on the treasure ship, why not put the bait there?"

"Sounds good," said Roger. "But how'll we catch him?"

"We'll slip back to the ship as soon as Mom and Judy are asleep and keep watch from behind the big dune near the ship. When he shows up, we'll jump out and catch him in the act."

"Great," said Roger, without much enthusiasm, "I hope he's not too big a ghost."

Soon they were on their way to the pirate ship. They placed the food in about the same spot they had found the tin can with the map in it. Henrietta wanted to stay with the food, but they made her return to camp with them.

A few minutes after they were back, the station wagon pulled in. The report on Bill was good. He would be able to leave the hospital day after tomorrow.

Chuck questioned his mother eagerly about the details of Bill's accident.

"Well, he remembered stepping over the driftwood log and hearing the rattle. Before he could locate the snake, it had bitten him. But . . ." She stopped and frowned.

"What, Mom? Who brought him a blanket and gave him first aid and killed the snake and made the shell trail?"

"I don't know. He didn't seem to want to talk about that part. Just said he 'passed out' and didn't know what happened after he was bitten."

"Anyway, he liked my flowers," broke in Judy. "He made the nurse put them in a glass and said they made him feel like a little bit of the island was in the room with him."

"The doctors are amazed at how quickly he is recovering," Mrs. Merritt smiled. "He has been bitten before, and is quite proud of his 'immunity.' "

"Poor Uncle John and Aunt Mabel," said Mrs. Merritt. "They're still having problems from wind damage caused by the storm. Mabel is frantically making preserves and jelly out of the peaches and plums that were blown off the trees in the backyard. And Uncle John is struggling through a mountain of paperwork connected with the insurance claims for damage to the roof."

"They wanted us to spend the night with them," said Judy.

"Yes, I've been thinking on the way back here that maybe we should go in tomorrow evening. I could help Uncle John with the paperwork, and the next day we'll be bringing Bill back anyway."

"Could Rog and I stay here with Henrietta?" asked Chuck.

"Hm-m-m, I don't know about overnight by yourselves. Let's decide what to do tomorrow." Mrs. Merritt stood up. "Right now I'm going to do some work on my notes."

Long after Judy was asleep Mrs. Merritt worked at her card table. It seemed she would never go to bed. Finally she put her work away. "Thank goodness," thought Chuck. But then she picked up a book on the Indian tribes of Texas and started to read.

The boys played cards half-heartedly as they waited and waited and waited. They began to think they would never get back to the trap on the pirate ship.

When they were about to give up, Mrs. Merritt called to them that it was time to turn in. For once in their lives they agreed.

"I'm afraid the ghost will have come and gone," Roger whispered.

"Me, too," said Chuck.

At last the light went out in the other tent. Impatiently waiting another fifteen minutes to give Dr. Merritt time to fall asleep, the two detectives finally set out. Roger carried a small flashlight.

Henrietta was settled for the night on her blanket outside their tent. She raised her head as Chuck and Roger crept past her.

"Good girl. You stay here," whispered Chuck, patting her. Apparently she decided she had had enough for one day and curled herself back into a ball and went to sleep.

The landscape looked unfamiliar in the darkness. Layers of clouds passed in front of the moon. Only occasionally did it come out to light their way. However, they had been to the old ship so often they had little trouble finding the way in the dark.

As they came closer to the ruin they began to hear noises. "Sounds like thunder," said Roger.

"It's more like growling," said Chuck. "Wait a minute." He stopped by a large pile of driftwood and debris. "Let's get some weapons, just in case."

Each of them selected a strong stout piece of wood. Then they continued cautiously toward the old ship skeleton. The sounds became louder. They seemed to be a mixture of rumbling, growling, whining noises.

"Keep behind that dune, and let's see what's going on." Chuck touched Roger's arm and nodded in the direction of a dune about fifteen feet from the old wreck.

Clutching their sticks tightly, the boys crept silently around the side of the dune so that they had a view of the scene.

"Oh, no!" exclaimed Chuck.

On the shipwreck, snarling and snapping at each other, were four coyotes fighting over the remains of the bait. Chuck and Roger watched silently for a few minutes.

Although they were making lots of noise and seemed to be saying ugly things to each other, the boys noticed that the animals avoided actually touching each other.

"They sure fit the saying of the bark being worse than the bite," said Roger, laughing.

"Right. But there goes our trap," sighed Chuck as one of the larger coyotes ran off with the last bit of silver foil hanging out of his mouth.

He shook back the lock of hair from his forehead. "Never mind. That means the ghost didn't get the food anyway. Maybe he's still hungry. Let's set out some more bait. Only this time we'll put it right in camp where we can keep a better watch."

Back at camp, they soon had more leftover fish and cornbread arranged on a piece of foil. Chuck placed it on a table that was set up a little distance from the tents.

He whispered to Roger, "The ghost ought to like that. It's in the dark, but the foil shines so he can't miss it if he comes looking for something to eat."

"Yeah," said Roger. "Now all we have to do is keep watch for him."

"Do you want me to take the first watch?" asked Chuck.

"I guess I'd better," answered Roger. "I'm pretty wide awake now, but once I get to sleep I'm hard to wake up again."

"I know!" Chuck nodded.

Roger spread a blanket to sit on in the dark shadow of the tent. From there he could see the table clearly, but he himself was almost invisible against the wall of the tent.

It seemed to Chuck that he had barely closed his eyes when he awoke to find Roger bending over him shaking his shoulder. "Come on, Sleeping Beauty. Your turn. I've watched for an hour, and we haven't had a nibble."

Chuck stumbled out of the tent and plopped himself on the blanket. Hard as he tried he couldn't keep his eyes from falling shut.

He tried saying the multiplication tables but he got stuck on eight times nine and nodded off. He jerked his head up and began to say the Presidents of the United States in order but dozed off trying to remember if Tyler came before or after Polk.

He decided to review the story of Tom Sawyer to try to keep his mind awake. He had read the book so many times he knew the story by heart. He was half-thinking, half-dreaming about the scene in the cemetery where Tom and Huck see Injun Joe commit a murder.

Suddenly his head snapped erect, and his eyes popped wide open. Something was gliding silently away from the camp table!

The sound of Roger's heavy breathing came from the tent. It would take too long to wake him. Chuck sprang up and raced after the dark shadow.

As he ran the thought came to Chuck that the shadow looked

like the "pigmy" he had glimpsed their first night in camp.

The small figure darted between the dunes like quicksilver. When Chuck followed it to the right it suddenly was revealed by the shifting moonlight to be to the left of him. As he zigged to the left, it zagged to the right. Then all at once it was behind him!

"It's like trying to catch one of those trick balls that take crazy bounces!" thought Chuck.

For a quarter of an hour the chase went on. The ghost appeared to be enjoying the game. Finally, with a gesture that looked like a wave, the small shadow flittered away for good.

Disgusted, Chuck returned to the tent. "Can't even catch a pint-sized ghost," he muttered.

As he passed Henrietta he saw that she was awake and watching him. But she hadn't stirred from her blanket. "Thanks, pal. You're a great help," he said.

He decided not to wake Roger. There was nothing more they could do that night. Besides, it would be morning in a few short hours.

chapter 12

NEW FACES

Tired from their midnight prowlings, Chuck and Roger slept late the next morning. Chuck opened his eyes a crack when something cold and wet touched his arm. It was Henrietta with her front paws on his cot, nudging him with her nose. Dr. Merritt stood in the tent opening drying off with a towel.

"Are you fellows going to sleep all morning?" she asked. "Henrietta and I have already been for a swim. I didn't wake you because you were sleeping like a couple of logs." She gave a final rub to her curly hair. "I'll rustle up some breakfast while you get dressed."

By the time they had each finished a huge stack of pancakes swimming in butter and syrup, Chuck and Roger were fully awake.

When Dr. Merritt said they were running low on butter and milk, they volunteered to walk to the little supply store for them. Henrietta watched Judy settle down to build sand castles by the water's edge and decided she preferred to go with the boys.

As the boys approached the store they noticed a black panel truck parked in front of it. It obviously had seen better days as a delivery truck. Now it was battered and covered with dirt that looked as if it had been there a long time. The only decoration on the panels was a sticker in one corner showing the picture of a skull and crossbones.

Inside the store were two young men paying Mr. McCline for two cartons of beer. The taller one had long, blond hair. They were dressed in tank tops, blue jean shorts, and sandals.

As Chuck and Roger walked around the dairy case to pick up the butter and milk, they heard the men questioning Mr. McCline.

"Now, Pops, we want to talk to this old sailor with the hook, see? We're from the museum like we told you, and we need to get some information from him," the taller one said.

"Yeah," said the blond stranger. "We understand he's been here forever and knows all about Indians and pirates and buried treasure and things like that."

The storekeeper shook his gray head. "Well, I don't know, but I guess you're referring to Mr. Bill Jones. I'm afraid you can't see him just now unless he's come home from the hospital in Corpus. You see, he was bitten by a rattlesnake a few days ago."

Mr. McCline was a kindly old man, usually very friendly, but he looked as though he'd be happy when these customers left.

Catching sight of Chuck and Roger he said, "Here are two young fellows now who might be able to tell you something. It was their family that found Bill after he was snakebit and took him to the hospital."

Chuck and Roger said hello to Mr. McCline. Chuck could barely keep from drawing back as the taller stranger laid a hand on his arm.

"How about it, Bud? You know anything about the old guy?"

He answered as the stranger tightened the clutch on his arm. "We don't know exactly when he'll be coming back." Chuck squirmed out of the stranger's grip.

The shorter man had a nose that looked as though it had been squashed in by a rock. He spoke in a slow drawl. "Now, ain't that nice of your family to take such an interest in a poor old sailor? Maybe he's promised to give you some of the treasure he must have found since he's been here such a long time?"

"Of course not," said Chuck angrily. "We're just friends.

Besides, I don't believe he has any treasure except maybe a few coins he might have picked up."

Chuck turned away from the two young men to pay for the milk and butter. In his haste he accidentally pulled one of his four-real pieces from his pocket along with the change his mother had given him.

Before he could pick it up both men moved forward to examine it.

"Well, now," drawled the shorter man. "It sure would be nice to take a few of those back to the museum. Could you just tell us about where you came across that coin, sonny?"

"Why—uh—it was just—uh—lying in the sand near our camp after the rainstorm," stammered Chuck.

The black-haired man gave his partner a frown. "Yeah, we know that these storms often uncover things that have been buried for years. That's why the museum sent us out to see what we can find for them after the big blow a few days ago."

As the two strangers left the store they passed Henrietta, who was waiting outside. She gave a low growl. The smaller man swung a pack of beer at her. "Who you trying to scare, fat dog?"

When they were out of hearing, Roger laughed in relief, "Good riddance. It's lucky Judy didn't hear that last remark!"

"Sure is," agreed Chuck. "I don't believe those characters were from any musuem. Do you, Mr. McCline?"

The storekeeper scratched his head with the pencil he kept behind his ear. "No siree, I do not. They're scavengers. Always get a few like them after a storm. Too lazy to do their own beachcombing. Rather take what somebody else has found than do their own hunting. A new breed of sand pirates, I call them!"

V-room. V-v-v-room. The black truck pulled away from the store with its motor roaring. Mr. McCline looked after it unhappily. "Hope that's the last we see of that pair," he said.

On their way back to camp the boys discussed the unpleasant meeting. "I wonder when they last had a bath," Roger commented.

Chuck grinned. "Whenever it was, it was too long ago. But, listen, let's not say anything about them to Mom or Judy. We've got to stay here on Padre tonight. It may be our last chance to solve the mystery. We'll be going home in a few days, and I just can't bear to leave without finding out about the ghost."

As they ate lunch, Mrs. Merritt told them she had decided they had better go back to Corpus that afternoon so she could help Aunt Mabel and Uncle John with the canning and paperwork.

"Please, Mom, can't Roger and I stay here? We wouldn't be any help, and our time here is almost over," Chuck said.

Dr. Merritt hesitated, and Roger spoke up, "Aunt Lucy, I'm sure we can manage just fine by ourselves for one night."

"Well, with Roger's level head and Chuck's know-how, the two of you should be able to handle any situation that arises," said Mrs. Merritt.

"And don't forget Henrietta," said Judy. "She'll be their lookout."

"Especially if we're attacked by clams or crabs," added Chuck.

A little later the station wagon was packed and ready to leave.

Just before they drove away, Dr. Merritt gave Chuck a key. "This is the key to the padlock I put on Bill's door. I didn't get to go to the cabin today. Will you and Roger go over there this afternoon and give Mr. Bones fresh water and fill his seed dish?"

"Sure," said Chuck.

"And please check to make sure everything is shipshape for Bill's return tomorrow," she added.

"We will," the boys promised.

Judy stuck her head out of the car window. "And Henrietta, you take care of the boys. And don't go off and fall in any holes. And don't chase the gulls too much. And don't sniff any crabs or jellyfish. And . . ."

Mrs. Merritt laughed. "That's enough for her to remember,

Judy. We'd better get going."

The boys watched until the station wagon became a tiny speck and then disappeared.

Chuck's eyes roamed over the vast, empty beach on each side of them and the great rolling Gulf that stretched as far as he could see in front of them. For a moment he felt a slight sinking feeling. Then he turned to Roger and grinned.

"Well, here we are."

"Yeah, here we are," agreed Roger calmly. "What are we going to do about it?"

"We're going to catch a ghost, that's what!" answered Chuck. "Tonight we'll set the bait on the pirate ship, and we won't leave it until the ghost shows up!"

"O.K. with me," said Roger. "But I think I'll catch a short nap now if we're going to stay up half the night again."

So for a while Roger slept, and Chuck tried to rest. But his thoughts were too busy to let him fall asleep. Surely tonight they would uncover the mystery that had hovered over them since they came to Padre.

This just had to be the night. But would this day ever end? After a restless hour Chuck couldn't stay still a minute longer. He shook Roger awake.

"Come on, Rog. Let's go feed Mr. Bones. At least it's something to do to make the time pass."

Roger yawned and looked around grumpily for his glasses. "Don't see why we need to rush. It's still early in the afternoon." In a few minutes his good humor was restored by a glass of milk and an apple, and he was ready to leave.

This was the hottest day since they had come to the island. Henrietta's tongue was hanging out soon after they began their walk. All three were glad to get to the cabin.

"It'll feel good to get in out of the sun," said Roger.

"That's strange," remarked Chuck as they came up to the door. He pointed to the padlock that Dr. Merritt had put on the door.

It looked as though it had been smashed by a heavy object and was dangling from the hoop that had secured it. The door itself was slightly ajar.

"Come in, come in," Mr. Bones called. Pushing the door open the two boys, followed by Henrietta, stepped hesitantly inside. For a moment they were speechless. Bill had often told them that he kept his house like a ship—a place for everything and everything in its place. But now!

"Wow! It looks like a hurricane plowed right through the middle of the room," said Chuck when he had caught his breath.

"Sure does," agreed Roger. He picked up some of the scattered arrowheads. "Watch out for the broken glass." He pointed to where some of Judy's "Christmas balls" lay broken into bits.

"Whoever it was sure did a good job of searching for whatever he was searching for. What a gosh awful mess!" Chuck looked around at the piles of personal belongings that had been dumped out of the cabinets and sea chests where Bill had kept them neatly stored. Even the dishes and pots and pans had been pulled out and thrown on the floor.

"Guess they got his coin collection." Roger held up the carved wooden chest that Bill had shown them so proudly a few days before. Now it was empty of the coins it had held. Even the lining had been ripped loose.

A sudden thought made Chuck hurry over to the inside door. Sure enough, the lock on it was broken, too. "Come on, Rog," he called. "At last we can find out what was behind the locked door."

chapter 13

UNWELCOME GUESTS

Quickly Chuck grasped the handle of the door and jerked it open. He and Roger looked intently around the small room.

There was another hammock, just like the one in the larger room. Against one wall stood an open sea chest with its contents flung out on the floor. They consisted mostly of undershorts, regular blue jeans, cut-off blue jeans, and T-shirts.

A small handmade table and chair that looked as though they were made out of ship's timbers stood against another wall. And that was all the room contained.

"Gee," said Chuck in disappointment. "If there were anything valuable in here, the robbers must have taken it."

"Yeah, it looks like it," agreed Roger. "But I wonder what Barnacle Bill used this room for. Why would he need two hammocks?"

"I don't know," said Chuck, who was examining some clothes that were hanging on a hook on the back of the door.

"Say, Rog, look here!" He pulled the clothes from the hook. "Barnacle Bill could never get into these jeans or this shirt!" Chuck held the garments up against himself. It was clear that even he wouldn't fit into the small clothes.

"Maybe they belong to your pigmy," Roger chuckled. "I can't imagine anyone else who could fit into them."

"Well, they just might. And they just might be the beginning of the answer to the mystery." Chuck tossed his hair out of his eyes and glanced at Henrietta. She was sniffing at a dark stain on the floor and whining.

He was glad of a chance to change the subject. "What do you suppose that spot is? She's been sniffing at it ever since we came in this room."

Roger's dark head and Chuck's sandy one brushed as they bent over the dark, reddish-brown spot. Slowly they raised their heads and stared at each other. Chuck spoke first.

"You know what it looks like?"

"Yeah, but . . ."

"Blood!"

"I know, but . . ."

"That's why Henrietta's been sniffing and whining." Chuck touched the spot. "It's still damp!"

"You know what that means?" Roger's face looked pale in spite of the tan he had picked up in the last few days.

Chuck nodded slowly. "Whatever happened—must have happened not very long ago."

"Right," said Roger. "And I vote we get out of here—right now!"

"No, we're not." Chuck glanced around at the littered cabin. "We told Mom we'd get things ready for Barnacle Bill, and that's what we're going to do. Blood or no blood." He began to pick up the scattered clothes and blankets. He folded each item and placed it back in the sea chest.

"O.K.," said Roger, beginning to pick up also. "But let's hurry!"

The two boys had never worked faster. In a matter of minutes Barnacle Bill's personal belongings had been replaced in the sea chests and cabinets, the arrowheads and other artifacts were back in their places, the floor had been swept clear of litter.

As he hastily swept the larger room, Chuck noticed several more reddish-brown spots. These were smaller and seemed to lead to the front door. He decided there was no need to call Roger's attention to them at that moment.

Cocking his head on one side, Mr. Bones watched the feverish activity with his bright eyes. He seemed to enjoy the performance they were putting on. From time to time he requested, "A little drink for Mr. Bones?" Getting no answer, he asked, "What's up, mate, what's up?"

When they had done all they could to restore the cabin to its usual neat condition, the boys turned their attention to the inquisitive parrot.

"Let's get his seed and water and get out of here," said Roger.

"Wait a minute. Both his dishes are full. And the water seems fresh," said Chuck in surprise.

"How can that be? He hasn't been fed since your mother was here yesterday. And you know he's eaten since then," said Roger.

"Look for yourself." Chuck pointed to the feeding dishes.

"Well, I just can't believe that anybody who would break in and tear up the place like this would be nice enough to take the trouble to feed a bird." Roger shook his head.

"Who else then?" Catching a gleam in Roger's eye and afraid that he was about to make another reference to pigmies, Chuck hurried on. "Let's go. We've done all we can here."

The padlock on the front door could not be made to work, so Chuck carefully pulled the door to. Then they hurried down the strip of sand outlined by shells that served as Bill's front walk.

"Now what's Henrietta found?" asked Roger.

"Looks like tire tracks," said Chuck as they came up to where the black dog was busily sniffing in the sand in front of the cabin.

"They lead off in the direction we're going, so why not follow them?" suggested Roger.

"Fine with me," answered Chuck.

Henrietta seemed to have the same idea. In fact, she had already set off along the tracks, looking back impatiently to see if they were coming.

In a few minutes the boys found that the tracks turned sharply toward the hard-packed sand along the edge of the beach.

"They can't have been made very long ago." Roger pointed toward the Gulf. "The tide's beginning to come in and they haven't washed away yet."

When they had walked another ten minutes and were getting close to their camp, Chuck started to say that whoever
made the tracks must have driven right past their camp. But
he stopped and pointed instead.

"The tracks turn right into our camp. And Henrietta's barking at something. Hurry, Rog!"

Both boys rounded the last dune at a run. There in front of
their tents was the dirty black panel truck that had been
parked in front of the grocery that morning.

Standing beside Mrs. Merritt's cooking table were the two
men who had questioned them about Barnacle Bill. Henrietta
had startled them, and they were both staring motionless at
the yapping dog.

"Bet they were after food," whispered Chuck.

"Yeah—and anything else they came across," Roger whispered back. "We'd better not make them angry. They probably
could get real mean!"

Chuck nodded quickly as they approached their unwelcome
visitors.

"Well, well," the tall young man spread his lips in a grin. "If
it's not our little friends from the grocery store."

The shorter man smiled crookedly. "Hope you're more
friendly to company than your hound is," the intruder said.

"Oh, she doesn't mean any harm. She's just protecting our
camp." Chuck stroked Henrietta. "Relax, girl." Reluctantly,
and without taking her eyes off the strangers, she stopped
barking and lay down.

"Mind if we set a minute?" said the dark-haired man.
"We've been hunting for Indian stuff and buried treasure for
the museum all day, and we sure are bushed."

Chuck glanced at Roger. "I'll just bet I know where you've
been looking, and it wasn't on the beach!" he thought.

Without waiting for an invitation, the strangers seated
themselves in two of the canvas chairs in front of the tents.

"My name's Stash," the dark-haired man said. He jerked his
thumb at the other man. "That's Bo. Now what's your names,

fellows?"

"Chuck Merritt."

"Roger Merritt."

Crossing one leg comfortably over the other, Bo asked, "Just what does your father do, Roger?"

"Oh, my father is an accountant. But we're not brothers; we're cousins. It's his mother and sister we're with." Roger pointed at Chuck. "And his mother is an anthropologist."

"Why, sure," said Stash. "That must be mighty interesting." He turned to Chuck. "Why don't you tell us about some of the things she does?"

Usually Chuck enjoyed talking about his mother and her work. But he didn't want to talk to these uninvited guests about anything.

He looked helplessly at Roger, who nodded slightly. Seeing no way out, he described as briefly as he could his mother's studies of various groups of people and their habits and customs.

When he came to the Karankawa Indians that Dr. Merritt had come to Padre to study, Stash straightened up from his sprawling position. "Listen to that, Bo, that sounds like some fun." He made Chuck tell over again about the cannibal practices of the Indians.

Both men questioned the boys repeatedly about their acquaintance with Barnacle Bill. They seemed convinced that he had hoarded treasure. Chuck and Roger had to deny over and over that Bill had ever given them any hint of having such a treasure.

When Chuck had about decided that they would never leave, Bo jumped up suddenly. "Hey, what's that dog doing— sniffing round our truck?"

He ran toward the truck waving his arms and yelling, "Get away from there, you!"

Stash followed him to the truck. "Don't get so uptight, man. What can a stupid dog do?"

Bo looked sulky. "I don't care. It's got no business messing around our truck. Let's go."

"Aw right, I'm coming," said Stash. "We have to take care of that unfinished business we started."

Without so much as another glance at their hosts, the two men climbed into the truck and zoomed away.

Roger laughed in relief. "I've never been so glad to see anyone leave. I don't care whether they say 'thank you' or not!"

"Wonder what was in their precious truck that they were afraid Henrietta would discover?" said Chuck.

"Huh—uh. Here they come again!" Chuck felt his heart jump as the roaring sound of the truck's engine grew louder. He closed his eyes in thanksgiving as it raced on past. "Guess they just turned around."

"You know, I don't feel comfortable just knowing they're on the same island with us," said Roger, looking at the sun that was beginning to set.

"Me, either. And . . . but maybe I shouldn't say anything." Chuck stopped and looked thoughtful.

"Oh, come on. Now you've said that much, you have to tell," said Roger.

"Well, I'm not positive, but I thought I heard some noises in side the truck in between Bo's yelling."

"What kind of noises?"

"It's hard to say. A kind of thumping, I guess."

"Maybe that's what Henrietta heard too."

"Could be. Anyway, something inside there made her curious."

"You know it just had to be those two that tore up Bill's cabin." Roger looked at Chuck over the glasses that had slipped down on his nose.

"I know," agreed Chuck. "I don't believe they're any more from a museum than I am."

"Did you notice the bandage on Bo's left hand?" asked Roger. "I'm sure he didn't have it this morning."

"Yeah, I saw that. Wonder how he hurt it?" Chuck patted Henrietta absent-mindedly. "Well, we'd better get busy if we're going to arrange a confrontation with Mr. Ghost."

"O.K.," agreed Roger. "Let's get supper ready. I'm glad we'll be busy tonight so we won't have time to worry about what our new 'friends' are doing."

"Right," said Chuck, as he watched the last rays of the sun reflect on the waves.

chapter 14

MODERN CANNIBALS

Before long the boys were sitting by a cheerful fire, eating pork and beans and canned ham, and talking over their plans to set another food trap on the old pirate ship.

"This time we'll stay right there on the spot and keep watch," said Chuck.

Roger yawned. "Hope it doesn't take too long. You got me up from my nap before I was ready, and I may not be able to stay awake long." Stretching, he got up and began to clear away the dishes.

"A nice piece of ham ought to appeal to a hungry ghost," said Chuck, wrapping the last of their supper in a piece of foil.

Taking along the bait and a small flashlight, they set out for the old ship. Henrietta, who had thought they were settled for the night, looked at them as if she wondered if the trip was necessary. When she saw they were really going, she scrambled to her feet and trotted after them.

A few yards from the ship, Chuck switched off the flashlight. Silently they crept up and quickly laid the shiny foil package in plain view. Then they scurried behind a dune.

"Where's Henrietta?" whispered Roger.

"I don't know. I thought she was right behind us." Chuck looked around. "Here she comes now. Probably been off chasing a sea gull or something."

"Come on, that's a good girl." Roger patted the sand beside him. "Lie down and be quiet now."

But it seemed Henrietta had something on her mind, and it

was not lying down and being quiet. She began to bark and circle around them.

"Aw, Hen," said Chuck, "this is no time for fun and games. Come on, settle down." He tried to reach out and touch her collar, but she backed away from his grasp.

She continued to run in bigger circles around them, occasionally darting off a little way in the direction from which she had come.

"She's trying to get us to follow her," said Chuck.

"Probably wants to show us a dead crab. She's going to ruin our trap with all that noise," said Roger in disgust.

"Listen!" Chuck held up his hand. "There's another noise besides Henrietta's barking."

"Sounds like somebody yelling or singing," said Roger doubtfully.

"Maybe that's what has Hen all worked up."

"Do you think we should go see what it is?" asked Roger with a sigh. He knew that Chuck's curiosity would make it necessary for them to investigate such an unusual noise.

"We might as well," said Chuck. "I don't think any respectable ghost is going to show up here tonight with all the racket that's going on."

Following Henrietta toward the source of the noise, they became puzzled. A rhythmical beat like a drum sound seemed to accompany the noise. The sounds themselves began to sound like a chant.

Roger touched Chuck's arm. "Do you know what that sounds like?"

"Yeah, but I don't believe it." Chuck stared at Roger. "Indians!"

Chuck put his finger to his lips and began to crawl on his hands and knees up the last dune between them and whatever was making the noise.

For a few seconds he couldn't believe his eyes. Then he had to clap his hands over his mouth to keep from bursting into laughter. Roger was stretched out beside him utterly speechless, and Henrietta also seemed stunned with amazement.

Chuck gripped her collar firmly.

Before them were the two strangers, Bo and Stash, stripped to their shorts. Their faces and bodies were daubed with red and black paint. Bo was beating on a pot with a stick, and both of them were yelling what they seemed to think were Indian cries as they leaped around a bonfire. Stash was waving a knife.

The sight of these make-believe Indians made Chuck feel like bursting into laughter. Then his eyes became adjusted to the light and he could see beyond the fire.

He felt his stomach tighten into a knot, and he no longer found the scene funny. On the other side of the fire, tied to a stake, was a small Mexican boy, his eyes huge with terror.

In a few minutes it became obvious that the Indian show was being staged for his benefit. As Chuck and Roger watched, Stash came close to the small captive. Waving his knife under the child's nose, he threatened to cut it off and roast it in the fire if he refused to "talk."

The prisoner shook his head and spread the fingers of his hands in a gesture that said that he didn't know what they wanted him to tell.

Paralyzed with horror, they watched as Bo rushed up to the small boy and grabbed him by the ear. "Now you'll tell where the old guy buried the treasure, or I'll whack this off for sure," he snarled, pulling out his own wicked-looking knife and waving it under the captive's face.

The little boy rolled his eyes helplessly.

Henrietta, who had been growling low down in her throat, bayed the deep call that the basset hound uses on the hunting trail, broke loose from Chuck's frantic grip, and raced headlong toward the blond man.

Bo released his grip on the boy's ear and whirled to face the angry dog.

"So, it's you, you pest. I'd just as soon cut your gizzard out, too!" He aimed his knife at the throat of the dog, who was jumping at him trying to find a place to sink her teeth.

At the sight of the knife threatening Henrietta, Chuck lost

his caution. He found himself on his feet running into the circle of light, yelling at Bo.

"You leave that dog alone!"

He heard Roger pounding right behind him.

"Umph," Chuck felt himself clutched from behind in a grip that squeezed the breath out of him.

"Got you!" Stash tightened his grip as Chuck struggled to free himself.

Chuck saw that Bo had stopped Roger with the knife that he now waved threateningly at him.

"Well, Stash, what'll we do with this nosy pair?"

"I don't know. You'd think they'd have better manners than to go visiting where they're not invited," Stash replied.

The corners of Bo's mouth moved a little upward. "I have an idea. Why don't we roast and eat them? The one you got might be a little stringy, but this one looks pretty juicy." Both laughed gleefully.

Chuck looked at Roger and formed the words "sick joke" with his mouth.

Unexpectedly, the little captive cried out, "No, no, señors. You cannot do that. They are my friends!" He took the threat seriously, and his face was twisted in distress.

"Oh, ho, so you can speak when you've a mind to," said Stash. "Well, you'll just see what happens to your friends if you don't tell us the truth about the treasure in a hurry! Let's tie 'em up, Bo."

"Wait a minute. First make him tie the mutt." Bo tossed some rope to Chuck. "Tie her good or watch us make her into hot dogs." He grinned sourly at Chuck.

As he fashioned a muzzle and then tied her feet, Chuck whispered soothingly to Henrietta. "Don't worry, girl. It's just for a little while. We'll figure a way to get out of this. I know we will."

In a few minutes both boys were tied hand and foot, lying in the sand.

"Now, which one will we cook first?" Stash scratched his head.

"Why don't we let their friend decide," suggested Bo.

"Yeah. That's a good idea." Stash stuck his knife under the little boy's nose again. "You tell us which one to cook first. And be quick about it."

The child shook his head violently. "No, no! Let them go! I'll tell you where the treasure is!"

"Not so fast. *First*, you tell us where the treasure is. Then we find the treasure. *Then* we let them go. And maybe you, too, if you tell the straight truth. Right, Stash?"

"That's mighty right. First the treasure. Then we talk about letting you go."

"I tell you now, señors. The treasure is buried in a chest in Señor Barnacle Bill's backyard. It is five feet from the yucca plant that grows there. But I can't remember in which direction from it."

"Yah-hoo! That's close enough. Come on, Bo. We're about to strike it rich. Let's get this lot in the truck and away we go!"

Roughly they hauled the three boys and the dog to the truck and tossed them in the back with no regard for skin and bones.

"Ow," yelped Roger as Henrietta landed on his stomach.

"She couldn't help it, Rog," said Chuck. "It felt like you cracked a rib when you hit my chest."

The back doors slammed shut, and the truck engine roared. With the noise of the engine and the partition between the front and back sections of the truck, the boys were able to talk without being overheard by their captors.

"How about telling us what this is all about," said Chuck to the Mexican boy. "Who are you? And how in the world did you get in such a fix?"

"And why did you call us your friends?" asked Roger.

"Si, si, I tell you from the beginning," answered the boy. "My name is Pepe Casas. My parents died when I was a baby. So I went to live with my grandfather. He was a very important man—the captain of a shrimp boat. I was his first mate. He let me help him in everything. Then came the big storm—almost as big as the one last . . ." Pepe's voice broke off.

"Gee, Pepe. I'm sorry. Don't tell that part if you don't want to," said Chuck.

"I want to tell you. It's just that I still miss him. We had engine trouble and got caught in the heavy waves. I was trying to help get the nets in, and a monster wave came and pulled me out of the boat."

"Didn't you have on a life jacket?" asked Roger.

"Oh, si. Grandfather always made me wear one. But the wave must have knocked me out. I don't remember anything else until I woke up in Señor Bill's cabin."

"He found you?"

"Si, he pulled me in like a fish and pumped the water out of me. He has taken care of me since then."

"Then those were your clothes in the back room. But why did he keep you hidden?"

"We were afraid the authorities would take me away from him and put me in a home for children without parents. So we promised each other not to tell anyone. He was so good to me— like my grandfather."

"But, Pepe. Maybe your grandfather did survive the storm," said Roger.

"No," said Pepe sadly. "Señor Bill went to Port Isabel, but there was no trace of him. I have no one now but Señor Bill."

"Ouch," grunted Roger. "I think my back is breaking."

"We've turned off the beach road. This truck must have four-wheel drive. We're riding over the dunes now," said Chuck. They all squirmed to get in the least uncomfortable positions to endure the jolting.

"Pepe, tell me," asked Chuck, "were you our ghost?"

Pepe giggled. "I confess. I am the ghost. I heard you call me that. Am I not a good ghost?"

In spite of their discomfort, Chuck and Roger laughed. "You were a great ghost. You really had us in a tailspin," said Chuck.

"And such a generous ghost," said Roger. "Say, where did you get all that stuff you put in the treasure chest?"

"Oh, don't worry. It was all mine. Some of it I found, and some of it Señor Bill gave to me. He did not care what I did with it. And after you found my pirate ship, I decided to help you have another pirate game by making a map for you to follow."

"But why did you want to give it to us? I still don't understand," Roger persisted.

"I don't know if I can explain very good. It's just that you are such a happy family. When I watched you in your camp I—almost—felt like I was a part of your family." Pepe's voice sounded shy. Then he laughed and added, "And I like the señora's cooking so much. And Henrietta and I have been amigos from the day you arrived."

"That's right, you were the pigmy she was with the first night," said Roger.

"Did you leave a note for Bill at the Indian campsite?" asked Chuck.

Pepe giggled again. "Si, it said 'Pepe was here.' He warned me to be more careful after that."

"And it was you, of course, that gave him first aid when the snake bit him," said Roger.

"Si, my grandfather taught me how to do that. I got that old snake, too. Then I made the shells for you to follow. I knew you would help him."

"We must be almost to the cabin. Hurry and tell us how you happened to be in the spot we found you in tonight," said Chuck.

"These two uglies came to the cabin about noon. I hid in the back room. But they broke the lock on the door. I tried to keep them from destroying Señor Bill's things, but they just knocked me out of the way. They kept talking about finding treasure."

"Yeah, they've got that on their minds all right," said Roger.

"We're slowing down," said Chuck. "Tell the rest quickly."

"I told them I didn't know anything about hidden treasure. But they said they would make me tell. Then they started to drag me off. That's when I bit the blondie."

"Good for you," said Chuck. "That accounts for the blood on the floor."

"We're stopping," said Roger. "I'm sorry for Barnacle Bill, but I guess it's a good thing for us that you finally told them where to find the treasure."

"But," said Pepe, "I didn't. I don't know where is any treasure. I just made that up to keep them from cooking you."

"Oh, good grief!" said Chuck.

At that moment the back doors were yanked open.

chapter 15

A DASH FOR FREEDOM

"O.K., Santa Anna," said Stash as he roughly pulled Pepe out of the back of the truck. "You're going to be the General in charge of this expedition. And if it ain't successful, just remember what's going to happen to you and your two amigos."

"I'll untie his feet so he can walk," said Bo. "What'll we do with the rest of this crew?"

"Leave 'em here. That way we won't have to watch 'em. They can't get into any mischief, hog-tied and locked in here."

"Holy cow! What are we going to do?" Roger said as soon as the doors were slammed and bolted. "They'll *really* be mad enough to kill us all when they find out that Pepe tricked them."

"We've got to find a way to get help. It'll take them a while to dig in a circle five feet all around that cactus. Think you can work your hands or feet loose?"

"No—the knots are too tight. How about you?"

"I've loosened the one on my wrists, but I can't undo it. My knife is in my back pocket. But a fat lot of good that does us."

"Hold on," said Roger. "I've got one of my arrowheads in my left back pocket. If you've loosened your hands maybe you can work it out."

"Yeah, and we can saw the ropes with it. Roll over on your right side and let's give it a try."

"Easier said than done," muttered Roger. Wiggling and squirming, he worked to turn himself so that his left jean

103

pocket was within Chuck's reach.

Henrietta gave a moan of protest. "Sorry, old girl, didn't mean to squash your tail," apologized Roger.

At last the boys worked themselves into position so Chuck could fish the arrowhead out of Roger's tight fitting jeans. "It was a tough fight, man, but I won," said Chuck as he finally managed to secure the arrowhead. "Now flip over, and I'll work on the rope on your wrists."

"Flip is right," groaned Roger. "I know how fish must feel when they flop around trying to turn over without any hands or feet to help them." When Roger had managed to reverse his position so that they were face to face, Chuck went to work on the ropes that bound Roger's hands.

After ten minutes of sawing, he stopped to rest. "Think I've gone through about half the fibers, but it's tough going, and my hand has a cramp in it."

"If you can cut through a few more strands, maybe I can pull the rest loose," said Roger.

"O.K., here we go again." Chuck resumed his sawing. "You pull while I cut." Another ten minutes of hard work and Roger's hands were free.

He rubbed his wrists. "That feels great. Now let me get your knife, and I'll cut you loose in a jiffy."

"Do Henrietta first. She doesn't understand what's going on, or why I tied her up in the first place," said Chuck.

Roger quickly removed Henrietta's muzzle. Then he began to cut the ropes that tied her feet. "Hey, stop licking me; I'll never get finished."

After Roger had freed Chuck's hands and feet, he cut his own ankles loose. For a few minutes they sat rubbing their wrists and ankles and enjoying the sensation of being able to sit up and move their limbs again.

"Next question," said Roger, "how do we get out of here? I heard them bolt the door from the outside."

"Let's try some foot power," suggested Chuck. "We'll both lie down with our feet against the door. We'll draw our legs back while I count three. Then when I say 'go' kick the door as hard as you can."

"O.K.," said Roger. "Let's try it."

In a minute they were lying in position, feet braced against the doors. "One-two-three-go!" said Chuck. Both boys kicked with all their might. But the doors remained shut.

"I think I heard that old bolt give a little," said Chuck after three more tries. "Come on, here we go again."

After half a dozen more "one-two-three-go's," the doors were beginning to bulge, and the bolt was obviously bending.

"We're getting there," encouraged Roger as they stopped to rest. "Let's make the next one an all out super kick. Ready? O.K., one—two—three—go!" On "go" the rusty old bolt at last gave way and the door flew open.

"Hallelujah! We're . . . uh oh."

"What's the matter, boys? Need a little fresh air?" Stash leered in at them. "Just thought I'd check and make sure you was comfortable."

Chuck glanced around quickly. Bo was nowhere in sight. He thought, "He can't handle all three of us by himself. It's got to be now or never."

Yelling, "Jump, Rog, jump," he leaped from the truck. Surprised, Stash made a grab for him. Chuck twisted his arm out of the man's grasp ripping his shirt sleeve as he broke free.

As he raced away he called, "Come on, Rog, run." But Roger was slower than Chuck. The now alert Stash caught him with no trouble.

Henrietta needed no urging; she was right on Chuck's heels. Hearing Stash calling to Bo for help, Chuck knew he had to keep on going. "Come on, girl," he said as they scrambled over the soft sand. "You and I have got to get help fast. Let's head for the hard sand where we can make time."

As they hit the edge of the beach where the going was faster, Chuck wasted no more breath in talking. Henrietta seemed to understand the urgency of their trip. Together they raced along the gently lapping water as fast as they could make their legs move.

When they came within sight of McCline's grocery, Chuck

put on a fresh burst of speed. Too breathless to call, he pounded on the locked door. But the door remained shut.

"My gosh, I forgot it's past midnight. Bet they've been asleep for hours," he thought. Running around to the back door, he pounded and Henrietta barked. Still no answer.

Catching his breath, Chuck called, "Mr. McCline, Mr. Mc-Cline. Please wake up. Please, Mr. McCline. Wake up! Wake up!" He was almost sobbing in his need to make the storekeeper hear him. Several minutes crept by.

Then a light spilled out from under the door, and it was pulled open. In his highly excited state the sight of the little old couple framed in the doorway imprinted itself forever on Chuck's mind. In the future he would be able to close his eyes and see every tiny detail of the scene.

Mr. McCline was in his pajamas. His sparse gray hair was rumpled, and he was fumbling with his glasses. In his half-awake state he couldn't get the frames over his ears. Mrs. Mc-Cline was peering over his shoulder. Her hair hung down her back in a long braid. She was groping to fasten her bathrobe—an impossible job, since she had put the robe on backwards.

"Why, it's the Merritt boy," exclaimed Mr. McCline. He finally managed to get the glasses hooked over one ear. "What on earth?"

"Please, sir, please! We've got to get help quickly! They may kill Roger and Pepe!"

"Wait a minute. Come in, son. Roger is your dark-haired cousin with the glasses, but who is Pepe? And who's going to hurt them?" Mr. McCline stepped back and beckoned Chuck and Henrietta inside.

"Why, you're completely winded, and so is your dog." Mrs. McCline bustled over to the sink. "I'll get you a glass of water."

"Thanks." Chuck took a few sips of water, a couple of deep breaths and shook the lock of hair out of his eyes. Then he hurriedly explained about Pepe and what had happened that night.

"My, my! Who would have thought young men from a museum would act that way?" said Mrs. McCline, shaking her head.

"Aw, Mother, I told you those two had never seen the inside of a museum," said Mr. McCline. He was busily looking for a number in the phone book. "Doggone, I almost forgot." He ran his hand through his rumpled hair and stared at Chuck in dismay.

"What's the matter, sir?" asked Chuck, wishing the little man would hurry and call the Rangers.

"Our phone is still out of service. Has been since the rainstorm knocked out the lines."

Chuck stared at him blankly. The precious minutes were slipping by.

"Tell you what." Mr. McCline straightened his glasses and his shoulders. "We've got to get reinforcements. I'm going to get the pickup and go after the Rangers!"

"But, Papa," objected Mrs. McCline, "if you drive by the cabin they'll hear the engine. And maybe they'll do something desperate."

"Already thought of that," said Mr. McCline, pulling on a pair of pants over his pajamas. "I'm not going to the station on the island. I'll go to the one in Corpus just over the causeway. Shouldn't take very long. Won't be any traffic this time of night."

Throwing on a shirt and cap, he hurried out the door calling to Chuck, "Wait here, son. I'll be back with help before you know it."

A minute later he burst back through the door, looking sheepish. "Forgot my keys for the pickup."

"Guess he's a mite out of training," said Mrs. McCline as the sounds of the truck engine died away in the distance.

She turned her attention to her two guests. "Now let me see what I can find for you two to eat. You must be starving after all you've been through tonight."

But Chuck couldn't eat. His throat felt too tight to swallow, even if his stomach wanted food. Henrietta, however, graciously accepted the leftover roast beef that Mrs. McCline offered.

Now that Chuck had his wind back, he began to feel like a caged animal. He couldn't stand not knowing what was going on. He just had to get back to Bill's cabin.

Mrs. McCline did her best to persuade him to wait for the return of Mr. McCline and the Rangers. Finally, she saw that he was determined to go.

"I wish you'd stay. But I can see you're bound to go. But, first, promise you'll only watch from a safe distance. Promise, Chuck?"

"Yes, ma'am," said Chuck, "I promise." Behind his back he carefully crossed the fingers of his left hand. He didn't like to deceive the kind woman. But he had to get back, and he knew he might not be able to just stay hidden and watch if things were going badly for Roger and Pepe.

Leaving Henrietta in Mrs. McCline's care, he set off for the cabin. This time he ran more slowly and easily so he wouldn't arrive at his destination completely winded.

As he jogged along, a plan was forming in his mind. He was trying to recall the details of a movie in which some criminals had been captured.

"It just might work," he thought. "In the movie they were in the water. But if I can figure out a kind of switcheroo, it might just work."

chapter 16

STRANGE FISH

As he came close to the cabin, Chuck heard angry voices. Cautiously he crept close enough to peer around a dune. The clouds had cleared and in the bright light of the full moon, he could see every detail of the scene.

Roger had been made to dig. Pepe was kneeling in front of the big cactus with his hands still tied. Frustrated and nervous, Stash and Bo were viciously threatening the little boy.

"What kind of a dirty liar are you?" growled Stash. "I don't believe there's a scrap of treasure in this yard."

"Yeah," said Bo. "You punk." He slapped Pepe hard on one cheek and then on the other. Tears came into Pepe's brown eyes, but he didn't make a sound.

"That does it," thought Chuck. "I can't just stand here and watch them beat Pepe up. Got to try my plan."

Making a wide circle to keep out of sight of the yard, he edged around to the front of the cabin. Silently he began unfastening the heavy fishing nets that were strung on the walls of the cabin.

"Can't toss them up on the roof," he thought. "They're too heavy, and anyway, they'd make too much noise. Guess I'll hoist them up with me."

Tying the end of one net around his waist, he struggled up on the two coils of rope he had stacked together. By grasping the overhang and straining with all his strength he managed to swing one leg up on the roof.

Tightening his muscles, he pulled the rest of his body up. For a few minutes he lay still, breathing hard. Then he sat up and began yanking on the net, pulling it up hand over hand. Finally it was all beside him on the roof.

"One down, two to go," he muttered under his breath. Twice more he repeated the performance. Now he had three of the nets on the roof with him.

The next step was to get them over the peak of the roof onto the roof of the lean-to. One by one he tugged them—up and over. Squirming on his stomach he pulled them to the edge of the lean-to's roof.

"These nets must weigh a ton. Now I know where Bill got his muscles," Chuck thought. He lay still a minute to rest and to study the scene below him.

Roger was digging close to the lean-to. The bullies were still over by the cactus with Pepe. Stash was holding Pepe by the hair. "This is it, Santa Anna," he snarled. "Game time is over. Either open up, or we're gonna take this nice shiny hair clean off your head."

"Yeah," said Bo. "And if you don't think these knives can do it, watch this." Grasping a clump of Pepe's hair he sliced it off with a swish of his blade.

Chuck wasted no more time watching. Quickly he reached into his pocket and fished out the two old Spanish coins that had been in the treasure chest that Pepe had hidden for them.

Roger had his back to the cabin. Carefully Chuck tossed the coins so they landed just in front of his surprised cousin.

As Roger looked up in astonishment, Chuck motioned him to silence. He held up the end of one net and motioned Roger to get the two men to come over close to the edge of the lean-to. Roger nodded his understanding.

"Hey," he called, "Stash, Bo, look here. Look what I found."

Stash and Bo whirled around. "Say," Bo began, "who told told you to dig way over there?"

"Shut up," snapped Stash at his partner. Dropping Pepe, he hurried over to Roger, followed by Bo. "What you got, kid?"

"I don't know," said Roger, holding the coins up close to his glasses and pretending to study them.

"Give them to me!" barked Stash, snatching the coins from Roger's hand. He stared hard for a minute, then showed them to Bo. "Looka there. That's the real thing all right."

Grasping Roger's shoulder roughly, Stash shook him. "Now suppose you show us just exactly the spot where you found these here coins, owl eyes."

Moving to a spot directly under the edge of the roof where Chuck was waiting, Roger pointed. "Here, this is where they were. Right here."

Both men fell on their knees and started digging with their knives in the spot Roger indicated.

Motioning Roger to move back, Chuck inched forward to the very edge of the roof. To his dismay a board creaked. But he needn't have worried. The two treasure seekers were completely absorbed in their work.

Grasping one net firmly in the middle, Chuck stood up. He leaned forward, counted three, and flung the net with all of his strength.

At that moment, a ball of black fur hurtled toward the hoodlums.

"Hey, no, Hen!" shouted Roger, but it was too late. Alarmed, the bullies jumped up, dropping their knives. Henrietta and the net hit them at the same time.

"Oh, my gosh," Chuck thought as he hoisted the second net. "She got away from Mrs. McCline. Can't be helped now." He dropped the second net. It landed squarely on the three struggling captives.

"And one to make sure," said Chuck, dropping the third net.

"Somebody get this mutt out of here. It's trying to kill me!" Stash bellowed.

"Yeah, yeah, get this mad dog out of here!" yelled Bo.

The more they thrashed around the more Henrietta barked and snapped at any part of their anatomy she could reach.

While Chuck was sliding down from the roof, Roger freed Pepe's hands. "Mil gracias, amigo," said Pepe. "I was getting pretty tired of being tied up like a Christmas package."

Roger and Chuck and Pepe shook with laughter at the sight

of the two bullies and the black dog jumping around in the nets.

"Those are the strangest fish I ever saw!" said Pepe.

"And the noisiest!" added Roger.

"Bo's right. Henrietta is mad. In fact, that's the maddest I ever did see her in my whole life," said Chuck.

"Come on, now, you're not mean kids. Get this hound out of here," begged Stash.

"Yeah," said Bo. "Before somebody gets hurt."

"Tell you what," said Chuck. "Since we really aren't as mean as you, I'll help you. It wouldn't be safe to try to get Henrietta out of there. But if you stay very still and let Roger ease those knives out of there, I think I can quiet her down."

"O.K., O.K., we'll be still. Make her lay off," said Stash.

"All right, Hen. That's enough. Easy, girl. Settle down." While Roger gingerly removed the knives, Chuck reached through the nets to pat the angry dog. Under his hand she lay still, keeping a sharp watch on her fellow prisoners and growling low in her throat from time to time.

"You've done a fine job, old girl. Now you're the guard," Roger told Henrietta.

He and Pepe settled themselves on the outer corners of the nets while Chuck sat near Henrietta to keep her calm. Stash and Bo stayed still.

"Now all we have to do is wait for Mr. McCline and the Rangers," said Chuck, yawning. "It's been a long night. Hope they hurry."

"One more little thing," said Roger to Stash. "You might hand over those two coins of Chuck's you stuck in your pocket."

Without a word the hoodlum handed the coins through the net.

"Won't Judy be mad to have missed all the fun?" said Roger.

"Right," said Chuck. "She probably won't be able to think up a word long enough to express her feelings!"

Five minutes passed, and then Pepe said, "I think I hear the sound of a motor." In another minute a station wagon with the

Ranger emblem on its side pulled up.

Mr. McCline and two Rangers jumped out. One of the Rangers was a tall, black man. The other was stocky and red-headed.

When they saw the net and its contents, they both burst out laughing. "That's got to be the weirdest haul I've ever seen," said the red-headed Ranger. "How about you, Steve?"

"Check, Joe," said the tall Ranger. "And I've seen some strange catches in my day. How did you land them, fellows?"

"Yes," said Mr. McCline, turning to Chuck. "Mother was worried about you and the dog, too, when she got out through a loose window slat."

"Well," said Chuck, "I had to come back to see about Roger and Pepe. I guess Henrietta felt the same way. You see . . ."

"Mr. Ranger," called Stash. "Let me tell you how it was. We were just playing a kind of game with these boys. And they took us serious."

"Yeah," said Bo. He struggled to get into a sitting position. Henrietta growled, and he subsided.

"Hm-m-m. That's interesting." With the help of his flashlight, Steve Jackson was taking a closer look at the two young men. "What's that red and black paint on you?"

"Oh, that." Stash gave a thin laugh. "Why that was just to make the game real. We were playing like we was Indians."

"Yeah," said Bo. "You know how boys like to play Indians."

"Well, I think we'll just let you explain the whole thing to the police in Corpus," said Joe Powell. "I imagine they'll be very interested in your 'game.'"

Steve glanced at his wristwatch. "Let's unwrap these prize fish and start back. On the way, you fellows can tell us how you caught them."

Joe brought handcuffs from a metal box in the back of the station wagon and put them on Stash and Bo as soon as the nets were removed.

Henrietta went wild with joy when the nets were lifted. She ran around frantically trying to lick the three boys all at once. Her tail was wagging so hard her whole body was shaking.

"Hop in, fellows," said Joe. He motioned to Henrietta. "You, too, old girl. You've done a good night's work."

On the way to Mr. McCline's store, Chuck and Roger told the Rangers everything they knew about the two men from the first time they saw them in Mr. McCline's store.

After dropping Mr. McCline off, the rest set out for Corpus Christi. Roger and Chuck rode in the front seat with Steve Jackson, who was driving. Joe Powell sat in the back seat between Stash and Bo, who didn't have a word to say the whole trip.

Pepe and Henrietta curled up on some rubber life rafts in the rear compartment. Soon both were sound asleep. Henrietta's snores provided an accompaniment for their conversation as Chuck and Roger told the Rangers what they knew of Pepe's history.

"And he thinks his grandfather was drowned in the last big storm before the one last week," Chuck ended the story.

"That would be about a year ago," said Steve Jackson thoughtfully. "Casas—somehow that seems to ring a bell. Let me do some checking. Maybe we can find out something definite. Poor little kid."

chapter 17

WHERE THE TREASURE WAS

After dropping off Ranger Powell and the "treasure hunters" at the police station, Steve Jackson drove the three boys to Uncle John and Aunt Mabel's. As they pulled into the driveway, he looked at his watch. "Three-twenty. Hope they won't be too startled."

Chuck had to ring the doorbell half a dozen times before John Miller sleepily answered it. His eyes popped open when he saw Chuck and Roger standing on the front porch. And even wider when he saw Steve Jackson behind them with the sleeping Pepe in his arms.

As Chuck was introducing the Ranger to Uncle John, the other adults, awakened by the noise, straggled in.

Aunt Mabel and Mrs. Merritt insisted on examining Chuck and Roger closely to make sure they were all right. They also did a lot of hugging and kissing that the boys put up with as patiently as they could.

After Pepe had been tucked into bed, Aunt Mabel made coffee and hot chocolate for everyone. She served it with big helpings of peach cobbler that Chuck and Roger devoured ravenously.

Steve Jackson stayed long enough to drink a cup of coffee with them and talk over the night's events. Then he left, promising to call back later in the morning to let them know if he was able to find any information on Pepe's grandfather.

Chuck and Roger had to tell the whole story of the night's adventure over once more before they finally went off to bed.

The last sound that Chuck heard was the snoring of Henrietta, who was sleeping on an old quilt at the foot of their bed.

The next thing Chuck knew his mother was gently shaking his shoulder. "Come on, son. You had better get up now. It's after eleven. I called the hospital and Bill can leave after lunch, so we need to get ready to go in a little while."

Chuck felt as though he could have gone on sleeping for another twenty-four hours. Gradually he stirred himself awake. It took fifteen minutes of shaking and pounding with a pillow and finally threatening to pour water on his head to get Roger out of bed.

Pepe had just awakened, too. The three boys were soon sitting down to a brunch of omelet, ham, biscuits, honey, orange juice, and milk. Aunt Mabel bustled about serving refills as soon as a clear spot showed on any of their plates.

While they ate, they told Judy again all the details of the night. "Darn it, Chuck always has all the fun. I miss all the important adventures," she complained. "Anyway, I'm glad Henrietta got to have a part in it."

Finally they convinced Aunt Mabel that they couldn't hold another bite. Judy fed the ham scraps to Henrietta. She and Aunt Mabel agreed that nothing was too good for such a "gen-u-ine heroine."

The doorbell rang as they were getting up from the table. Uncle John brought Ranger Steve Jackson into the kitchen. With him was a small gray-haired Mexican man of about fifty-five. He was neatly dressed in blue jeans and a yellow windbreaker.

Pepe took one look and knocked over his chair as he hurled himself into the stranger's arms. They were both laughing and crying at the same time. "Pepito, Pepito," was all the man could say.

"This is Pepe's grandfather, Señor Casas," Steve Jackson explained unnecessarily.

When Pepe and his grandfather could be persuaded to sit down, the Ranger continued his explanation.

Señor Casas had seen Pepe washed overboard by the huge

wave. Rushing to try to reach the little boy, he had cracked his head on a piece of rigging that the storm had broken loose.

For some time he had lain on the deck stunned. When he could move again, Pepe was no longer in sight. After searching for hours, he had given up, feeling sure that his grandson had drowned.

Señor Casas nodded as he listened to Steve Jackon's explanation. "Si," he said, "then with my heart sick with sadness I moved from Port Isabel to Port Aransas. I wanted to be in a different place—to help me forget what I had lost."

Then Pepe had to explain to his grandfather how Bill had fished him out of the water and taken care of him. "He was so good to me. Almost like another grandfather," said Pepe.

"Yes," said Dr. Merritt. "And it's about time we were leaving to pick up your other grandfather at the hospital. I'm sure he doesn't want to stay there any longer than he has to."

Half an hour later, Bill came limping down the hospital walk to the station wagon. "Mighty glad to see you folks," he said, shaking hands all around and giving Henrietta a couple of pats in exchange for her enthusiastic licks.

"I can never thank you enough for the care you have taken of my Pepito," said Señor Casas. "I have not the words to tell you what you have done for us."

"Aw, no need for thanks," said Bill gruffly. "I got a lot of pleasure out of the little tyke. Guess I knew it couldn't last forever."

On the drive to Padre they talked over plans. Bill invited Señor Casas to stay with him a few days in Pepe's room before they left for Port Aransas.

The old sailor tried to hide the sadness he felt at losing Pepe. But before they had crossed the causeway Señor Casas had invited him to come to Port Aransas as often as he wanted to work the shrimp boats.

"I have several boats now. And we always need help. A good sailor like you could have a steady job there," he urged.

Bill was not eager to give up his freedom, but he did promise he would come often to help and to visit.

Of course, Bill had to be told all about Chuck and Roger's adventure of the night before. He made Chuck repeat three times how he used the nets to catch the bullies and Henrietta's part in the capture.

"If that ain't the dangdest thing I ever heard," he chuckled. "Don't I wish I'd been there."

When they reached the cabin, he insisted they all come in. "There's something these boys has earned the right to know," he said. "It's true that over the years I've been around these parts I've collected a little bit of what folks call treasure."

"Ahoy, mates. How about a little drink?" Mr. Bones cocked his head at them.

"Ahoy, yourself, you old sand pirate," replied Bill. "Now you just behave yourself, and let's show the folks our little secret."

Reaching inside the door of the cage, he carefully pried up the floor of Billy Bones' cage with his hook.

"A false bottom!" exclaimed Roger.

Sure enough, the bottom lifted out to reveal an eight inch deep storage space. It was filled with old coins, pieces of jewelry, and modern money.

"So that's where the treasure was," said Chuck.

"I'm glad I didn't know about it," said Pepe. "I might have told the bullies about it to keep them from killing us."

"Well, if it'd come to that, I reckon I'd a heap rather have you safe and the treasure gone than t'other way around," said Bill. "Matter of fact, an idea just come to me. I never had no real use for this stuff before, but now maybe I do."

"Tell you what," he continued. "Would you like to look over the things in that cage?"

"You bet," said Chuck eagerly. Judy and Roger agreed.

"O.K.," said Bill. "You just poke around in it much as you like. I want each of you to choose a couple of pieces to keep. I owe you a heap more than that for all you've done for me."

Mrs. Merritt protested, "Oh, no, Bill, you shouldn't."

Bill held up his hook. "Ain't no use protesting, ma'am. You're dealing with a hardheaded sailor. Besides, there's one more favor I'm going to ask of you. I need some advice. So while

they're looking over the treasure and choosing, I'll ask you and Señor Casas to step outside for a little private gab."

Bill lifted the container filled with the treasure out of the cage and set it on a table. Then the adults stepped outside.

Jumbled together in the container were silver and gold pesos, pieces of eight, Spanish gold doubloons, Mexican real-pieces, old English and Spanish gold and silver coins dating back to the 1600s and United States silver dollars.

Mixed in among the coins were pieces of jewelry—heavy gold rings set with pearls and diamonds, a string of red coral beads, a few pairs of intricately made earrings, many single earrings, gold and silver bracelets and necklaces of many kinds, cameo brooches, and brooches with diamonds and pearls.

For a few minutes the children stared wide-eyed at this ancient Spanish treasure retrieved from the sands of Padre over the years by a pirate descendant.

"I'm going to choose the red coral necklace and a silver dollar," said Judy.

After much thought, Roger and Chuck each selected a silver piece of eight. In addition, Roger chose a gold peso, and Chuck picked out a gold doubloon.

Dr. Merritt stuck her head in the doorway. "Time to go back to camp. Bill needs to rest, and Pepe and his grandfather must have a lot of visiting to do."

"You will come back tomorrow?" asked Pepe.

"We'll bring a picnic and eat it in Bill's backyard," promised Mrs. Merritt. "And you and your grandfather walk over to our camp for a visit whenever you like."

"You bet," said Pepe. "Especially if you have brownies!"

Soon the Merritts were back in their camp. "What do you say we see if we can find our dinner out there in the Gulf?" suggested Dr. Merritt. Soon she and Chuck and Roger and Judy were knee deep in the surging waves. Before long they had caught half a dozen good-sized trout.

That evening after a meal of the fresh trout, they sat around a driftwood fire talking over the events of their visit to Padre.

WHERE THE TREASURE WAS

Roger and Chuck were sprawled on their stomachs on a blanket. Judy sat on a log, brushing the sand out of Henrietta's fur. Dr. Merritt sat in a camp chair.

"Would you all like to know what Bill wanted to talk with me about?" asked Dr. Merritt. "I don't think he'll mind my telling you, if you will keep it a secret for a while."

"Sure," said Chuck. "Did it have something to do with the treasure?"

"Yes, it did. He wanted to know how he could use it to help Pepe get a good education. I asked him if he was sure that was what he wanted to do with it. He said he'd never been surer of anything."

"What did you tell him to do?" asked Roger.

"Well, I suggested he get Uncle John's friend at the bank to help him. He'll probably advise him to turn it into a trust fund."

"I'll bet it's worth a fortune," said Chuck, who was examining his share of the treasure.

"Well, probably a small one," said his mother. "Anyway, he'll need legal help. I'm so happy that Pepe has a bright future thanks to the kindness of that good man."

"Yeah, he sure is soft on the inside to look so tough on the outside," mused Chuck.

His mother reached over and pushed Chuck's hair down over his eyes. "I believe you did learn something this trip."

"Only two more days," sighed Judy, "and then after we spend the weekend with Aunt Mabel and Uncle John, it's back home."

"Well, we're not going back empty-handed," said Chuck, tossing the hair from his forehead. "Seeing Bill's treasure and getting to pick out some for ourselves was the next best thing to finding treasure ourselves."

"And I've got a marvelous collection of shells," said Judy. "I've got sea biscuits, sharp eyes, baby's foot, sand dollars, angel wings, and jingle shells."

Dr. Merritt smiled. "You're getting to be a good conchologist, Judy."

"A who?" demanded Judy.

"I think that means you know a lot about shells," said Roger.

Mrs. Merritt nodded. "Yes, and I've got quite a bit of valuable information on the definite location of a Karankawa camp and will be able to direct an archeological team to it."

"I've got a good suntan for the first time, and I'm glad I've got my arrowheads and coins. And something else we haven't mentioned," said Roger.

"What's that?" asked Judy.

"Oh, I meant things to remember. Like last night. Guess we won't ever forget that, will we, Chuck?"

"You bet we won't!" Chuck said. "And we've got some new friends to remember, too—Bill and Pepe and Señor Casas and the McClines."

Mrs. Merritt was watching a sand crab scuttle away with a piece of orange peel someone had dropped. "Don't forget the other gifts nature gave us besides the sunshine—the sand, the surf, the wildlife."

"And the trout in our stomachs," added Judy. "I wonder what Henrietta will remember."

"Probably those noisy birds for one thing," said Roger, pointing to half a dozen squawking sea gulls who were diving for fish in the bright moonlight.

"And swimming in the Gulf and sliding down the dunes," said Judy.

"I'll bet there's one thing for sure," said Chuck. "There are two ex-treasure hunters who'll never forget Henrietta!"

At the sound of her name, the black dog lazily opened one eye and looked at Chuck. Before she closed it again the lid flickered up and down, exactly as though she had winked at him.